# The Danegeld

## By
## C.L. Hadyn

## Decadent Publishing Recent Releases

King of Her Heart by TL Reeve
So Not a White Knight by Starla Kaye
Treasure Me by Heather Long
Unexpected Gifts by Sarah and Shannen Brady
Out of Orbit by Thea Landen
Awake: Unsleeping Beauty by Louisa Bacio
If You Can't Stand the Heat by Taryn Kincaid
The Ambassador's Daughter by Venus Cahill
Safe at Home by Wendy Burke
Double Down by Desiree Holt
All I Want by Eden Ashe
Dressing Lily by Siobhan Shannon
One Night in Jersey by Tianna Alexander
Guardian of the Angels by Ashlyn Chase
Sorority Row by TL Reeve and Michele Ryan
The Vessel by Nancy Fraser
Return to Ecstasy by Tina Donahue
Beyond the Veil by Courtney Sheets
Blown Away: Detonate by D.L. Jackson
Blown Away: Explosive Affairs by D.L. Jackson
Downstroke By Desiree Holt
Conquer the Demon by Shiela Stewart
The Danegeld by C.L. Hadyn

# Also by C. L. Hadyn

Off Track

Hej dar! My name is Cyn Hadyn and I am of Hungarian and Swedish descent, and like my Hun and Viking ancestors, I have nomadic genes. Trust me, such peripatetic wanderings can wreak havoc on your English. However, my forays into foreign countries have come to an end and I now call Florida home. At least my last foray was swifter by Honda than Hun horse or Viking longboat.

I am very pleased to introduce another Scandinavian, Nels Kierkegaard. Nels is a complex character torn between family duty and wanting a life of his own. Fortunately for Nels, the ancient gods haven't abandoned him, and he meets the one man who can give him everything he desires. But the Scandinavian gods are capricious and won't award the prize unless he survives their trials.

# The Danegeld

Rosilyn Hugh de Lassy, a former Special Operator and now sole owner and operator of De Lassy Inquiries, can proudly trace his family tree back to the Normans who helped William the Conqueror win at the Battle of Hastings in 1066. Like his Norman ancestors, if Ross wanted something he went after it, and he wasn't afraid to work hard to get it.

When Nels Rainer Kirkegaard, possessor of a PhD in History, talented artist and skilled wood-worker, inherits his grandfather's furniture business, he is surprised by the stipulation he has one year to sow some wild oats before assuming the leadership of the company. In a chance encounter in a Washington, DC pub, Norman and Viking meet, and Ross surprises himself by hiring Nels to help him renovate the rundown monstrosity he intends to turn into office and living quarters.

When Nels' silver blonde hair and Arctic blue eyes make him the target of a sex slave ring, Ross is compelled to rescue him. He is very good at finding things, and no self-respecting Special Forces operator would leave a friend behind. However, while searching for clues to discover where his handyman was taken, Ross finds one of Nels' pen and ink sketches, and realizes the Dane could become more to him than just a friend. Ross has a major decision to make when he finds Nels. Should he, like his Norman ancestors, pay the Danegeld and live in harmony with the Viking or refuse and live at war with himself?

*Danegeld: A tax levied in Anglo-Saxon England from the 10<sup>th</sup> to the 12<sup>th</sup> century to finance protection against Danish invaders. A land tax levied as tribute to the Danish invaders.*

*To Irene Southwick, your enthusiasm is much appreciated.*

# Chapter One

"Sorry to make you trek out to the old homestead, Mr. de Lassy, but I thought it best to discuss this out of the office. Would you like something to drink before we get into the sordid details?"

"A finger of scotch would be welcome. I prefer it neat."

Roslin de Lassy waited as J.P. Morgan, no relation to the famous financier, splashed a generous, thick finger of scotch into the rock crystal glass. A man's glass, meant to be held in a powerful hand.

As Morgan fixed his own drink, the pock of a tennis ball hit with a certainty proclaiming skill in the sport attracted Ross to the wall of windows dominating the man's study. Two men, well, upon closer inspection, one man and a teenaged boy, engaged in a ferocious volley. From what little he knew of the sport, the man, who moved with the liquid slide and swing of a pro, dominated the court and seemed to anticipate where the boy would place the ball. Whoever he was ran the youngster to the edge of his physical stamina without noticeable effort on his own part.

The volley, and the match, came to an end with the boy's vociferous curse.

"Shit! You must have eyes in the back of your head."

Ross had to agree. He'd seen the boy place the ball right on the far court line, and the man run full tilt with his back to the net to return it to the far court on the boy's off side to catch the kid wrong-footed and clumsy. The kid's desperate return slammed the ball right into the net.

Morgan pointed to the tennis court. "My son and, believe it or not, his tutor. The man can play, and he's an even better academic teacher. Thanks to him, my son received a higher score on his SATs than we'd dared to hope for and got accepted by my alma mater. At the beginning of the year, I didn't think Junior's grades would get him into a trade school. Tennis is the first sport he's shown any aptitude for, and I'm hoping he'll try out for the tennis team."

J. P. pointed to one of the leather chairs before his desk and ordered, "Now, grab a seat and tell me who's been fucking with my company's web and how much damage they've done."

Ross took a small sip of the excellent scotch and

gave the bad news first. "Your hacker is a pimple-faced eighteen-year-old. The good news is, while the hacking has been inventive and annoying, we found no nefarious intent, and no company secrets broadcast to competitors. The kid's a techno-wizard bored out of his gourd working in the mail room. He spends most of his day playing high level games on your Internet and creating anonymous jabs to wound your pride."

Morgan drained his drink and slammed the glass down. "Well, I hope he has a handheld device so he can continue to play his games in the unemployment line."

Ross took a moment to peer out the window at the now empty tennis court. "Are you sure you want to fire him? Seems to me a kid with so much talent can be put to better use than distributing mail."

"Okay, I'll bite. What would you do with him? Make him a VP?"

While Morgan's suggestion smacked of sarcasm, Ross nodded. "Oh, he'll get there soon enough, but for now, I'd put him in charge of Web security. Who better than a hacker to know how to prevent hacking? Give him a small office and a title with commensurate pay increase and responsibility, and he'll work his ass off to keep your company secure because it'll be his company as well. No hacker wants another hacker pissing in his sandbox."

"I wish to God I'd hired you first, de Lassy. I spent a lot of money on another firm, and they couldn't find the source of those annoying emails to my private account. You've managed to find the little fucker in just one week, so I'll follow your advice. I'm also putting your number in my personal contacts in case anything else pops up. I'd be happy to recommend you should any of my associates need a firm that delivers discrete, on time results for a reasonable fee."

Ross laughed. "Well, I'm a firm of one at present, but new clients are always welcome. I have a certain knack for finding things.

Ross accepted the check from the man's hand, and they shook. He didn't glance at the amount; the CEO didn't strike him as a penny pincher. He hoped his prediction concerning the teenaged hacker turned out well for the company.

# Chapter Two

Ross returned to his Old Town Alexandria, Virginia, town house and stripped off his suit. He would've hung it in his closet if the closet, bedroom, and all the rooms on the second floor, including the floor itself, didn't need a complete overhaul. His town house had started out as two separate units, but since they'd been on the slippery slope to total condemnation, he'd gotten them for a song and the promise to live onsite.

The street he'd chosen to homestead on manifested a blatant air of urban decay, so his first repair jobs had been to paint over the gang graffiti and install a high, wrought iron fence with spiked top and keypad entry. A hair-trigger security system and bullet-proof windows gracing front and back made his place impregnable to all but the most determined criminals.

Ross hoped, once his place had been restored to pristine order, others would follow suit and begin the reclamation of the neighborhood. But until buyers could be persuaded to take a risk, he counted on his security measures to keep the gangs from tagging, breaking into, or shooting up his place.

At least he didn't have to stress over money. All those tours in the sandbox with his Army Compartmented Elements teammates earned him a boatload of dough with no place to spend it, so he'd invested with an eye to the future. Once back in the States, most of his buddies wasted their pay on fast cars and women, but his appetites lay elsewhere.

Hunting terrorists burned most men out around the age of forty, so he'd always had a contingency plan. But he hadn't planned on retirement kicking in ten years ahead of schedule due to a lucky shot from a Taliban gunman. And that's why he found himself standing in a room with peeling wallpaper and nowhere to hang his suit, but at least his company name graced the front door, and he had his first satisfied client under his belt.

Ross hoped today's meeting would lead to other jobs. The slow start at least gave him time to work on his living quarters. He'd knocked down the interior walls separating the two units and completed the first floor as his office and client meeting room right after signing the mortgage.

Ross stifled the urge to pat himself on the back

over the effect he'd created. The meeting space now felt like a private club rather than an office. Comfortable, butter-soft leather chairs and sofas of Scandinavian design set the room off and marked it as professional but relaxing. After discovering the original living room fireplaces worked, he planned on using them during the winter months to add to the club effect.

He countered his taste for spare, uncluttered design by selecting bright colors and rich fabrics to add warmth and eye appeal. Since the two town houses mirrored each other, he used one side for a client meeting room and the other for his private office. Once again, he chose Danish modern teakwood for the desks, filing cabinets, and bookcases. State of the art computers, and burgundy leather executive chairs completed the picture of a prosperous office.

Well aware of the initial outlay of cash, he couldn't help but cross his fingers each time he sat at his desk and hoped he established a name for himself before his nest egg tapped out.

Ross also believed in dressing for success. He'd purchased Armani suits, English oxford shirts, and the Hermes label graced his silk ties. The word sacrilege sprang to mind each time he had to hang his clothes on the nails he'd pounded into the mildewed and peeling wallpaper of the bedroom wall. A black T-shirt, paint-splattered jeans, and tool belt replaced the expensive clothes for the restoration work he needed to do today.

He'd chosen dark laminate wood for his bedroom flooring, and today he'd begin the installation. With any luck, he'd soon be able to spend his nights in his new bed with comfortable foam mattress instead of a sleeping bag atop an air mattress on the old, splintery floor.

He'd become such a regular at the Scansa Wood furniture store, they greeted him with open arms and expedited anything he ordered. By the time he finished up for the evening, he rivaled the teenaged tennis player in the amount of sweat dripping down his face, but he had a shiny, no-longer-warped floor to walk on.

Satisfied with the day's accomplishments, Ross was headed for a good, long, hot shower when his phone rang and he had to scramble to locate the damn thing under the mound of his sleeping bag. He'd flung it there to get it out of his way to lay the floor.

"Yo, Lassie, what're you up to? Gunner, Otter, and I are in DC for some 'please, sir, give us more money' time. We thought you might honor us with your august presence at our favorite Irish Pub, unless you're now hobnobbing with senators and congressmen, and have gone over to the Dark Side."

At the mention of the name Lassie, Ross could hear barking in the background. His former team couldn't be broken of their habit of calling him Lassie after the TV collie or, if in a hurry, shortening it to Dawg. No one in the team ever used his full name of Roslin de Lassy. Ross hated his first name. It sounded too much like a girl's name, thus he always referred to himself as Ross, but he took pride in his Norman-French heritage. His family had fought alongside William the Conqueror at the Battle of Hastings.

"As usual, Troll, your timing is impeccable. I've worked up a monumental thirst, so I'm up for meeting you guys. Give me a half hour to clean up, and the first round is on me."

"Well, you would've had to be here five minutes ago to buy the first round, but as we're all still thirsty, we'll let you buy the next. We might still be sober when you get here, but I'd hurry up. A man wants to blot a day spent begging from his memory with strong spirits."

Ross hung up the phone and started stripping on his way to the shower. It'd be good to see his old teammates again. Like his own surname, Troll was a play on the man's name, and it suited him. Captain Trollinger did appear troll-like with his large, muscular arms and legs, broad chest, and impressive height, and he relished scaring the bejeesus out of whatever ne'er do well crossed his path. But Troll showed his jovial side to his teammates and didn't need to be asked twice to help them out of a jam.

Separating himself from the team had been hard, but he had no regrets. He enjoyed being his own boss, and he also enjoyed not having to be called on to put on a dog and pony show for the politicians who thought they knew how to run the war in the sandbox better than the military on the ground.

"Well if it isn't one of Willie the Conqueror's boys come to wet his whistle," Troll called out when Ross entered the pub.

Ross took a seat and gestured for the waitress to set up another round of ales and shots of Irish whiskey. "How're you doing, Troll? Have you managed to find the perfect Trollette yet?"

When the man spluttered in mock anger, one of the others fielded the question.

"Ah, Lassie, you know Troll would need to blindfold the poor thing first. He's too ugly to find one any other way."

"I guess I've gotten used to his ugly mug. I so looked forward to seeing what kind of genetic mutants the two would breed. Hey, Gunner, how are those anger management classes coming?"

A standard team joke for the man they'd nicknamed Gunner for his proficiency with anything containing bullets. Gunner usually appeared to be half asleep until the team needed his expertise. Most of the targets they'd engaged would've loved to have kept him calm, but they no longer had breath to apologize for the error of their ways.

Turning to the remaining man, Ross reached across the table with hand extended, "Good to see you again, Otter."

The man thrived in water, especially when planting an explosive device of his own making on the side of a ship, or oil rig, or anything else Uncle Sam needed vaporized.

Ross picked up his whiskey when the waitress served him and stood to offer the toast. "To our fallen comrades."

Troll rose and lifted his glass as well, "Gone but not forgotten." Gunner and Otter chorused, "Never forgotten."

Ross regained his seat, and as he took the first sip of his ale, multiple ring tones sounded around the table. For one, brief moment, his heart rate kicked up, but he remained still as his former teammates listened to their messages.

"Ah shit, Lassie. We've got to go. There's just enough time to get back to our hotel and grab our stuff to make the next hop back to Bragg." Draining his ale, Troll stuck out his hand. "Well, at least begging fat-cat politicians for money has put me in the mood to go kill something. If you still remember which end of a rifle a bullet comes out of, why don't you join us up at the cabin this hunting season?"

"Sounds like a plan, Troll. You guys stay safe." It took a great deal of intestinal fortitude not to ask about the mission. He no longer had a need to know.

In the lull following his friends' departure, Ross's stomach set up a chiming of its own. He hadn't taken the time to eat today, and his gut told him it was amenable to eating whatever struck his fancy on the menu, dessert included.

Giving up his seat at the table, Ross headed for an empty stool at the bar and asked for a menu. He'd decided on a bowl of the pub's primo seafood chowder with accompanying soca bread when the man next to him asked himself a rhetorical question.

"Who eats seaweed in their salads?"

Ross turned to his neighbor and discovered the same man he'd seen beating J. P. Morgan's son at tennis. Sticking out his hand, Ross introduced himself, "We haven't met, but I saw you run J. P. Morgan's son all over the tennis court earlier today. My name's Ross de Lassy.

"While I can't say whether or not the seaweed salad is good, I can recommend the seafood chowder and soda bread."

"Thank you, I'll take your recommendation. My name's Nels Kirkegaard. Yes, I tutored his son and taught him tennis after his lessons."

Nels grinned and scratched the side of his nose. "Funny thing about tutoring. If you do your job well, you work yourself right out of a job. Do you work for Mr. Morgan?"

"I did. Like you, if I do my job well, I need to find new employment."

Ross, more to be friendly than curious, asked, "Are you seeking another tutoring job?"

"Not necessarily. I'll take anything that engages brain as well as body."

Ross's training enabled him to size up people fast, but with this man he got mixed signals. If you went by the hand-tied bow tie and button-down shirt, you got your classic academic. However, if you went by the hair, cut to look tousled. the faint hint of a beard, woodsy aftershave, leather bomber jacket, and hand-sewn half Wellington boots, you'd think metrosexual rich boy. Even the cuffs of his shirt sported embroidered initials.

Nels appeared to be a man who either didn't need to work or lived way beyond his means. He could pass for a professional model as well. Nels had hair so fair it shone like quicksilver, and his faint silver-blond beard, and lithe tennis-player body, had attracted the notice of the women seated across from them at the bar. If Nels didn't want to go home alone this evening, he wouldn't have to work too hard to find company.

Before he could engage his brain to run an acceptable word scan, Ross heard himself ask, "Can I buy you another ale?" *Sheesh, de Lassy that almost sounded like a pickup.*

When Nels accepted without giving him a fishy-eyed glare, Ross relaxed. "Too bad you aren't in the market for a woodworking job, I could use someone who knows how to lay floors, install cabinets, and do those kinds of finishing jobs."

Nels turned on his stool, the better to see Ross de Lassy. "I happen to be good at working with wood. My grandfather, a master cabinetmaker, taught me. I'd be most interested in helping you install cabinets and flooring."

Ross laughed, "About all I know about wood can be summed up with: measure twice, cut once, or it'll be damned expensive, and, yes, I found out the hard way. What would it cost me to hire you for your carpentry skills?"

Nels quirked an eyebrow and rubbed his chin. "Oh, I don't know, whatever you want to pay. I like taking jobs that interest me, and right now being a carpenter interests me. Umm, there is one caveat. I drink coffee, copious amounts of coffee."

Ross shook his head in disbelief. "Nels, you need to learn not to sell your woodworking skills short. I'll pay you the standard rate for a carpenter, and I'll provide the coffee, and throw in a donut or two if you're as good as you say you are."

After writing his address and phone number on a piece of paper from the pad he always carried, Ross handed it to the man. "Here's my address. I've a gated entrance, so press the intercom button and I'll buzz you in. If you show up by eight o'clock tomorrow morning, you're hired.'

Ross left the pub full of chowder and ale, still incredulous he'd hired a total stranger to help restore his new abode. If the man was as talented as he claimed, he'd have his place livable sooner than planned, but he'd damned well make sure Nels Kirkegaard demonstrated skill in carpentry before he gave him too much leeway.

# Chapter Three

Nels pressed the intercom button at the gate and flipped up the visor of his helmet to speak into the box. His grandfather taught him to be five minutes ahead of the appointed time to avoid being late. Nels grinned as he removed his helmet. His grandfather had said fifteen minutes, but since today happened to be a Saturday, Nels didn't want to arrive too early in case the man had slept in.

When he heard Ross's greeting, he identified himself and guided his bike through the open gate. By the time he swung his leg over the bike, Ross stood on the front steps.

"Sweet ride, Nels. Classic Ducati, if I'm not mistaken."

"Thank you. Yes, I discovered it in pieces in a back road garage, and I restored her myself."

"Hey, maybe we could ride together sometime." Ross hurried to explain. "I have a bike as well, although my Harley's too new to be called a classic. I've been too busy restoring this place to ride much, but it'll be nice to break away for a ride when it's no longer a choice of goofing off or having a bed to sleep in."

Ross stood back from the door. "Come on in. I'll show you around and explain what I have in mind for the renovation. Good to see you've come dressed for work."

Nels stared down at his paint-splattered jeans and work boots and laughed. "I like my leather jacket and dress boots too well to subject them to sawdust and wood glue."

As he followed his new employer inside, Nels glanced at the brass plaque to the right of the door. It featured a rampant lion with the words *de Lassy Inquiries* etched underneath. He wondered what type of inquiries, but the building before him caught his attention. The conjoined townhouses struck him as architectural classics built in the days when masons used genuine brick. Modern ones used a brick façade to save money. This structure was at least three stories and had towers at each end. The picture of having to cross a moat sprang into mind and made him grin.

As he followed Ross from room to room, Nels got a sense of what the man intended for his personal living quarters, and he agreed with his choices.

"I'm guessing you like modern furniture with a

strong emphasis on the Scandinavian style, all light woods and metal."

"Yeah, I do. I hate fussy furniture. Maybe I'm a throwback to my Norman-Viking roots. I doubt they had a lot of furniture in their castles, but what they did have was functional, and, I'd like to believe, comfortable. However, I intend to soften the starkness with warm colors on the walls and floors as well as in the textiles and artwork I use for accents."

Nels elicited a huge grin from Ross when he threw tact aside to say, "I'm hoping your design does not include reinstalling flocked paper. I will happily help you remove this bilious shade of chartreuse paper, and this gray linoleum floor in the kitchen, if that's where you want to start."

De Lassy really had a solid design. The two sides of the building would become a split floor plan with the master suite, to include a private study, on the left, and the guest rooms, dining room, and common great room would be on the right. With that configuration, Ross would still have his privacy with guests in the house.

Ross tore a loose piece of paper off the wall. "As much as I would like to see this itchy paper go, let's start with the kitchen. The sooner we get the island framed in and cabinets hung, the sooner I can have it measured for stone countertops. I've already purchased cherry wood cabinets.

"I hired professional plumbers and electricians." Ross pointed. "You can see where the outlets are, and there is running water. I had all the bathrooms ripped out and modernized right after I moved in, and while I could've done the plumbing myself, I wasn't crazy enough to mess with electricity."

Pointing to the stainless-steel percolator on the floor next to a large plastic cooler with a box of donuts on top, Ross added, "I made the coffeepot my first appliance purchase, but having an actual counter to set it on would be nice.

"I finished installing my bedroom flooring last night, and if we get the kitchen done next, I can order a bed and appliances. My mother was a gourmet cook and taught me to cook as well. I'd like to be able to cook in my own kitchen instead of eating out all the time."

Tapping a faded refrigerator-sized spot on the wall in front of them, Ross continued, "If the original refrigerator had been cleaned within the last twenty years, I might've considered keeping the relic until I could order a new one, but I discovered it to be a health hazard when I opened the door. I didn't want to swallow plague germs with my orange juice."

"Kitchen it is then." Nels had been staring at the outlets for electricity and water as Ross pointed things out, and picked up a piece of discarded cardboard and drew a quick sketch. "May I suggest the placement of the cabinets here and here, the counter angled this way to give you more efficiency when going from sink to workstation, and…" Nels stopped and glanced up at the ceiling. "You haven't told me what you intend for lighting in here, but if you say you're keeping this overhead light fixture, I'm afraid I'll have to quit."

Looking up to where Nels pointed, Ross laughed, "I see we're on the same page. I'm positive this fixture was ugly when brand-new in the eighties. I want track lighting I can angle to provide light where I need it. Pour yourself a cup of coffee whenever you want one, but let's get started. I like your suggestions, so why don't we start installing the cabinets on either side of where the refrigerator will be?"

Four hours later, Nels finished screwing the last screw into the last cabinet and Ross called a break.

"Man oh man, I didn't think we'd get this far this morning. I think we've earned a beer. Want one?"

At his affirmative response, Ross went to the large

cooler, removed two cold bottles of Corona, and slid down the wall across from where he sat on the floor.

"Sorry, no lime wedges, but at least it's cold."

"What do you want for lunch? There's an Italian place right around the corner that does great meatball subs. I can call it in and pick it up when it's ready."

"Yes, thank you. Subs sound good. I haven't tried a meatball, um, sub before."

"Okay, Nels. I'm guessing from your English accent and lack of experience with submarine sandwiches, you aren't native to the United States. Are you British?"

"No, Danish. I learned English when I attended Oxford University. I have a doctorate in history, so I speak English as well as Latin, German, Arabic, and Hebrew. The ancient historians I studied didn't always stick to English."

"You must have a real ear for languages to be able to handle all of those," Ross complimented.

"Perhaps, but I think it's more eidetic memory. Once I see or hear something, I can remember it. It's how I rebuilt the Ducati. All I needed was to flip through the manual, and I never had a problem assembling it."

"Wow, I'm impressed. Do you have any other

interests or hobbies?"

"Well, you know I play tennis, but for relaxation, I paint."

"What type of painting do you do? I mean, like landscapes, portraits, or modern art?"

Nels gave an exaggerated shudder, "No modern art, though I like modern furniture design. I'm a traditionalist. I do portraits or landscapes."

"I sketch in charcoal or pen and ink. I've been known to dabble in watercolor, but I prefer oils."

Before Ross could question him further, he asked a question of his own. "Could I rent your guestroom?" When Ross started to shake his head, Nels rushed on. "I think we could make a great deal more headway if I stayed here. Right now I'm in the Morgans' gatehouse, but since my tutoring job is over, I don't feel right staying there, even though they said I could remain as long as I liked."

"You can't be serious, Nels. My guest room has nothing in it but a working bathroom and a bare bulb for lighting."

Nels sweetened his ante. "Since anyone would be hesitant to offer a room in his house to a total stranger, let me tell you a about myself so you won't worry you allowed a criminal into your home. My full name is Nels Rainer Kirkegaard, and, sorry to say, no relation to the existental philosopher Kirkegaard.

"My parents are Wynter and Freya Kirkegaard. My father is the modern equivalent of a Viking raider, but now he uses a luxury Mercedes to conquer corporations rather than a dragon ship.

"My mother is an interior decorator. She met my father when he tried to take over my grandfather Rainer's furniture factory. You may have heard of it, Danegeld. My father didn't get the company, but he didn't come away empty-handed, either, as he married my mother right after his bid failed.

"I'm an only child, and, much to my father's disgust, I resemble my grandfather more than him. I have the same fair coloring and blue eyes as my grandfather, Rainer, but not his height. I'm six foot two inches. My grandfather stood six foot five inches in his slippers.

"Both of my parents are career-driven individuals, so they shipped me off to boarding schools almost as soon as my mother weaned me. I'm not close to my parents by mutual accord. During vacations and summer recess, I lived with my grandfather, and he taught me all I know about wood and design. Since he favored bow ties for some arcane reason, I wear them in his honor, despite their being a less than manly sartorial choice here in the States.

"When my grandfather died last year, he shocked my parents by leaving his company to me. Well, at least it will be mine when I turn thirty. The provisions of his will state I'm to travel and sow some wild oats before I knuckle down."

"Wow, I wish my grandfather had put such a stipulation in his will."

Nels laughed at Ross's comment. "Yeah, my parents were surprised as well. However, I think I'm genetically incapable of leading a frivolous life, so I seek out interesting temporary jobs. I came to the United States to broker a deal between Danegeld and your Scansa Wood stores. Even though I'm on holiday, I'm keeping a hand in Danegeld operations so I can hit the ground running when the time comes."

"I'm not sure your tutoring experience, or furniture manufacturing experience, is a good fit for remodeling townhomes, Nels, and I really know nothing about you, personally."

"The plaque on your door says you do inquiries, so I know you'll be researching me on the Internet, and I have no worries you'll find anything negative about Nels Rainer Kirkegaard."

*Now to raise the bid.* "Aside from helping with the renovation, I can also offer a significant discount on all Danegeld products, should you choose to purchase more. I've already noticed you have some of our furniture line in your office downstairs.

"For full disclosure, I should also include my faults. While I am artistic, I can't cook. Whenever I attempt to prepare anything edible, some sort of alchemy occurs, and it becomes, for lack of a better word, toxic."

He stopped his life story when Ross handed him a new beer to replace his empty.

"Well, Nels Rainer Kirkegaard, since you've taken the time to introduce yourself, I should do the same. "My name is Roslin Hugh de Lassy, and, for obvious reasons, I go by Ross. I come from the Norman-French line who fought with William the Conqueror at Hastings.

"As a historian, I'm sure you know how the battle ended. Although the de Lassy name isn't listed as one of the original fifteen companions, we received considerable land grants in England and Ireland after the battle.

"The family motto is *Meritas Augenter Honores*, which I know you can translate, but which I translate as, if you give me something it becomes mine, and I don't give it back without a fight."

"My parents are deceased, but I have one brother who lives in Tennessee and is working hard to ensure the de Lassy name carries on. I have three nephews and one niece, so far. Like you and your parents, my brother and I are not close, perhaps because he and I didn't see eye-to-eye on my former career. I served in Army special forces until I retired this year."

"Oh, I've read of Army special forces. You were a Green Beret, then?"

"Yes, but not exactly. I was a Green Beret serving with a part of the Army whose mission had nothing to do with winning the hearts and minds of people. When I met you at that Irish Pub, I was visiting with some of my former teammates."

"Ah, yes. I picked up on the military vibe. What made you leave the service, if you don't mind my asking?"

"Two reasons. The first of which was a bullet to the shoulder, and the second was I'd figured out what I wanted to do upon leaving the service. Since my command sent me to places where I couldn't spend money, even if I'd wanted to, I had a substantial nest egg to start my investigation agency and purchase this building. I'm hoping Mr. Morgan liked my performance well enough to recommend me to others because I really am very good at finding things that need to be found."

"My hobbies are cooking, so you are off the hook for that, mixed martial arts, and collecting edged weapons and old battlefield maps. I dislike being routinely beaten to a pulp by my martial arts instructor, watching golf on television, bad wine, and, now, I can add your cooking."

Nels laughed. "Yes, by all means add my cooking to your list. It truly is toxic."

"I'll tell you straight up, Nels, I'll be looking into your background, because I can't afford for you to compromise my fledgling business in any way. I'll also tell you I'm taking you up on the furniture discount. Why don't we start with the purchase of two beds, one each for your room and mine? At least, after a hard day of working on this house, you'll have a soft mattress to sleep on."

"It's a deal. What size bed would you like?"

"Make them both king. The rooms are large enough for them, and if they're the same, I won't have to buy two different sizes of sheets."

Nels nodded. "Do you like platform beds?

Danegeld has a new line, named after my grandfather Rainer. I can show you them on our website, and I'll use my executive discount on whatever you choose. I can have them delivered tomorrow, if that's okay?"

"Wow, I must've been in the right place at the right time when I accepted the Troll's offer of a beer."

"Troll?"

"Ah, sorry, it's team humor. He's last name is actually Trollinger, but we shortened it. While he's probably big enough to be a troll, he isn't nearly ugly enough. And lest you think I'm picking on him, my team name was Lassie, like the old TV series collie dog. Mine they usually just shortened to Dawg."

Nels cocked his head at the unusual nickname. "Although I've just met you, Dawg doesn't seem to fit."

Ross looked away and scratched his chin. "Can't say I'm sorry to lose that moniker. Ross de Lassy is more suitable for my new career.

"Those subs should be ready by now. I'll be back in ten. No, put your wallet away, I'm buying lunch."

Ross no sooner left the building than the phone downstairs started to ring. Since it appeared to be coming from the office line, Nels dithered whether to answer it or let it go straight to message. After the fourth ring with no interruption, Nels pounded down the stairs to answer the call, rather than have Ross miss out on a possible new customer. He made it down the stairs and to the phone on Ross's desk before the connection was broken.

"De Lassy Inquiries." He laughed to himself at the sentence. With his English accent, he sounded more like a butler than a secretary.

After listening to the man's request, Nels answered, "Sorry, Mister de Lassy is presently away from his desk. May I take a message? Yes, he should return within the hour, and I'll make sure he returns your call." He committed the man's name and number to memory and hung up the phone.

When Ross returned, he told him of the call. "I hope you don't mind, but I assumed you'd want to have the phone answered in case it was a new client."

"No, I don't mind. Thanks for answering it. I can use a new client or three to pay for these renovations. Um, I guess I'd better return his call now and see what he wants. Here are the subs. Don't wait for me. I don't think this will take long."

"As whatever is in that bag smells delicious, I won't wait. I also won't promise not to eat yours if you don't return by the time I've finished mine." Nels chuckled when Ross double-timed it down the stairs to his office.

He was back before he could swallow the first bite of his meatball sub. "Hey, I'd better still have a sub."

Nels failed to stifle a burp. "It wasn't in any danger. These meatball subs are huge…and messy. I hope you brought some napkins back with you." He grabbed the handful of paper towels Ross tossed him before settling on the floor to attack his own sub.

After swallowing a bite, he informed Nels, "Well I've got some good news and bad. That was a new client. He's coming over to meet with me at three o'clock today."

Nels finished half his lunch before asking, "I'm assuming getting a new client was the good part, so what's the bad news?"

"You'll have to wolf down the rest of your food, because we'll only have another hour to finish framing in the island before I have to shower and dress. Hey, while I'm meeting with my client, why don't you return to the Morgans and begin packing up your stuff? Move what you can today and finish up tomorrow."

"It won't take me long to pack my possessions. My Ducati is the largest thing I own. All the rest can fit in my duffel bag or be strapped to the bike. I travel light because I never know where I'll be going next after a job finishes up."

As he'd predicted, it took him less than two hours to return with his leather duffel and easel. He tried to be quiet as he entered, in case the new client hadn't left, but he needn't have worried.

When Ross met him in the entrance and saw his collapsible beech-wood easel, he made him an offer he couldn't refuse.

"The third floor of this place has a working bathroom and a skylight. You might want to paint up there. The light will be better than the window and bare lightbulb in your bedroom."

"Thanks, I'll take you up on that. What have you got mapped out for tomorrow?"

"Well, I plan to start on a new case which will take me out of town for a week or two. You can explore back roads on your bike or paint. Sorry to interrupt the work, but I can't be in two places at the same time."

Nels stuck his hands in the back pockets of his jeans and rocked on his feet as he asked, "Who says you can't? If you'll have access to a cell phone, I can continue the renovations and take photos of anything I'm stumped on, or any accessories I need to buy before I install them. If I keep working, this place will be farther along by the time you finish your inquiry."

"That's a fantastic idea, Nels. Let me give you a list of the appliances I want, and I'll give you my hardware and Scansa Wood credit cards to charge them. I've already run your name through more databanks than you'll ever hear about, so I have concluded you're as honest as you say you are, and, if I'm mistaken, I know how to find you." Grinning with a noticeable lack of humor, he added, "And I am very good at making you pay up when I do."

Nels smiled. "I can run but I can't hide? Don't worry. I have no intention of cheating you. This house has captured my interest, and I'd like to see it restored to *meisterwerk* level. Um, in case you don't speak German, it means masterpiece."

# Chapter Four

Ross sat behind the wheel of his dark-tinted SUV and studied the file he'd made on his new client. For the second week in a row, he'd parked down the street, and far enough away not to attract the attention of the residents of a fieldstone mansion owned by one Elmer Prinz, Hungarian-American, and owner of an electronics factory producing some miniature super whiz-bang part for the defense industry.

By the looks of the mansion, Mr. Prinz didn't have to worry about needing to go on welfare in this lifetime, but maybe, Ross mused, that wasn't a correct assumption at all.

The winter of Mr. Prinz's discontent centered on his third trophy wife, thirty years younger and nipped and tucked to preserve her youthful figure. Ross's binoculars confirmed no frown or laugh lines, and also noted grapefruit-sized breasts adorned the current wife.

Mr. Prinz had hired him to find out why Mrs. Prinz had become a constant drain on his wallet, and the financial deficit was too large to be attributed to even her excessive taste in clothing, jewelry, or furnishings for the house. Elmer Prinz suspected his wife might be cheating on him, and he'd be damned if he'd let his hard-earned money be lavished on some "rat-fuck gigolo." Mr. Prinz's expression, not his.

If he hadn't mastered the hurry-up-and-wait technique in the Army, Ross would've chafed at the present surveillance duty. He'd never cottoned to sitting behind the wheel of an anonymous vehicle, eating what he could grab at a fast food place for breakfast, lunch, and dinner, and then pissing in a wide-mouth, plastic juice jug because he couldn't leave to get to a toilet. He hoped something would happen soon, instead of wasting his time for a third week.

Getting calls from Nels on the progress he made on the renovations became a small respite from terminal boredom.

Ross kept three-fourths of his brain focused on the Prinz residence as he communicated with Nels via cell phone, to approve selections for furniture, appliances, and even door handles for the kitchen cabinets. He also thumbed through photo selections of paint swatches, area rugs for the bedrooms, and brochures of the Scansa Wood platform beds Nels wanted to purchase for his room and the guest room.

Maybe Nels's mother taught him a little something about interior design, but Ross had yet to negate any of his choices. With any luck, this case and his living quarters would have a simultaneous conclusion.

A panel van pulling into the driveway drew his attention, and Ross shut off his cell phone and raised the binoculars to read the sign, *Acme Pool Service* displayed on its side.

Funny, this appeared to be the second pool-service van in one week. The other had been from an agency called Sweet Water. He made a note of the man's appearance when the guy hopped out of the van and made a beeline for the gate to the back yard. He didn't carry any pool cleaning equipment like the Sweet Water guy had. Ross waited until he disappeared through the back gate before climbing out of his SUV and walking up to check out the van.

One peek into a side window, and Ross summed up the driver of the van as a pig on two legs. The front and rear seats gave ample backup to his assessment, covered with hamburger wrappers, empty beer cans, a mummified slice of pizza, and, most telling of all, a wadded-up lace thong.

The vehicle also lacked pool skimmers, chemicals,

spare hoses, or anything else associated with a pool.

Ross double-timed it back to his car to grab his long-range telephoto-lens camera and hyperbolic listening device. He'd bet his hockey season tickets the man performed a service, but cleaning pools wasn't it.

Ross used his ACE skills to get close to the pool without being spotted. When he drew close enough to use the camera and listening device, he flattened out and started recording and snapping pictures.

In less than a minute, Ross knew Mr. Prinz would not be happy reading his final report. So much so, he hoped he wouldn't kill the messenger. His camera recorded full-color images of a nude Mrs. Prinz snorting a line of cocaine from the bogus pool cleaner's equally nude body. His listening device also recorded the man's insincere regret to inform her she'd have to shell out more of Mr. Prinz's money for her recreational drugs.

When the woman began whining she couldn't afford to spend more or her husband might begin to suspect something, the Acme Pool Service representative offered a deal. If the missus agreed to come to a particular location each week, and party for a few hours with a select clientele, he'd keep the price of her drugs affordable, and she'd be home long before her workaholic husband ever knew she'd been out. As an incentive, the man offered a small bottle of MDMA, also called Molly, to help her party.

Ross's last two pictures showed the woman swallowing one of the pills and full penetration. He returned to his SUV and waited until the pool cleaner, aka drug dealer/pimp, swaggered back to his car.

Ross tailed him to two more stops in exclusive neighborhoods. If the man intended to do the same thing he did with Prinz s wife, he had to take his hat off to the dealer's stamina because, while the woman had used drugs enabling her to party with abandon, the man hadn't used any.

Before calling his client to say he had the information he requested, Ross snapped the license plate of the van. He felt bad leaving the man free to continue his illegal activities, but law enforcement wasn't in his job description. It would be up to Mr. Prinz how he wanted to deal with his wife and her adulterous addiction.

Meeting Prinz at his office, Ross seated himself and remained still while his client flipped through the photographs. Without prompting or a spoken word, Elmer Prinz listened to the tape Ross had made of the meeting between his wife and the drug dealer. By the end of the tape, Elmer Prinz had his head in his hands.

"Well, it's true, then."

"Sir?" Ross queried when the man didn't elaborate.

"It's true there's no fool like an old fool. I'll even include the other trite expression made popular by the Beatles. 'Money can't buy you love.' So this is what the fruit of my labor bought me. No wonder I couldn't find the source of the cash drain. I'd never have thought to look up her nose."

Ross could see the man held a tight rein on his temper, and he didn't want to say or do anything to let that horse out of the stable, so he remained seated and didn't offer any comment. He breathed easier when Prinz continued in a reminiscing voice.

"Maybe this would hurt more if, deep down, I didn't always know I'd made a rum deal. If I'd allowed my brain to overrule my ego, I never would've...."

Prinz couldn't quite meet Ross's eyes as he continued, "Right after I divorced my last wife, I discovered I had cancer. The urologist told me I needed to have my prostate removed if I wanted to continue living. I felt great after the surgery, but it left me unable to get an erection. At least I escaped the incontinence that sometimes occurs, but I couldn't escape the loneliness of being without a woman in my life."

*Whoa, too much information. Not necessary, not necessary at all. Waiter, check please.* Prinz, unaware of his discomfort, continued.

"I played fair and told the woman everything, and she agreed to be my wife and remain faithful to our marriage, which I thought she understood meant no outside affairs. And, in return, I would give her a lifetime of financial security way beyond her temp-hire lifestyle.

My factory had been short of secretarial staff, due to a flu outbreak, and she'd come to fill in for several days. Having seen her for yourself, I don't need to tell you she's a real beauty. I should've checked deeper into her background than I did, but I'd fallen under her spell. She made me think the lack of sexual congress between us didn't matter."

Poor bastard. At least, not being able to get it up ensured he wouldn't have to ask his doctor to check him for STDs or AIDS.

"What would you do, if you found yourself in my situation, de Lassy?" At the incredulous expression Ross gave him, Prinz clarified his question. "What should I do about my wife and the drug use?"

"Well, sir, you hired me to find the cause of your financial problem, which I did. As a single man, I'm not qualified to offer a solution to your marital problems, but for what it's worth, I'd say, if you can't reconcile her actions, I'd see to it she got put into some sort of rehabilitation program. I recommend you use one out of state so tongues don't wag, and then divorce her on the QT with a generous settlement to keep it out of the newspapers."

"But our neighbors...my colleagues will wonder where she went," the man protested.

"You can say she's traveling out of country, if anyone inquires, and by the time anyone asks again, you can tell them you've agreed to separate by mutual accord. As far as the drugs, ask your lawyer to broach the subject with the police to see to it Acme Pool Service is put out of business.

Prinz nodded. "And they can handle it from there, you think?"

"The narcotics branch of the police will do their own tailing of the pool cleaner and see who his source is. I would imagine, in return for the information you provide, your wife's involvement need not be mentioned."

Prinz sighed. "Good advice, de Lassy. I'll consider

41

it. I've wired your fee to your bank account as requested.

"Thank you, sir." Ross moved to stand but settled back in his seat when the man continued.

"Here's a piece of advice for you to consider, since you've told me you're still a single man. Sometimes growing old and being alone is not as bad as sharing your life with the wrong companion. You've got a few more years before you get to my age, so use them to choose wisely. Now, get the hell out of my office, and, not to denigrate the job you did, I hope I never need your services again."

Ross vacated Prinz's office without looking back.

# Chapter Five

Ross returned home intent on heading straight for the shower. The sordidness of Prinz's case made it mandatory, but when he climbed the stairs and got a gander at the finished kitchen, he stopped dead. His whistle of appreciation drew Nels from the guest room.

"Oh, you're back. I'd hoped you'd return before I went out. Let me show you what I've done in your absence."

"The kitchen looks fantastic, Nels. What happened to the black countertops? I thought we'd agreed on black."

"I know, and I did try to order it, but the man who came to do the measuring told me after he finished here, he had to go remove a black countertop he'd installed because the homeowner hated it. Her main complaint was, no matter how clean she tried to keep it, water spots made it appear dirty, and it was almost impossible to keep water spots from hitting the counter if she touched anything in the kitchen. I asked him if black counters did show water spots, and he said they did, so I made an executive decision and ordered the multi-toned brown granite instead."

"Thanks, you saved me a lot of money. I love to cook, but I can make a real mess while doing so. The brown goes better with this honey oak flooring, anyway."

Nels pointed over Ross's shoulder, "Why don't you check out your bedroom? I hope you like the platform bed. Mine is quite comfortable."

Ross walked into his bedroom and gaped. "When did you have time to do all this? Didn't you sleep at all while I sat in my car and kept watch on who went in and out of my client's house?"

Ross discovered his bedroom's ugly wallpaper had been replaced by lichen-green paint, which blended well with the dark-walnut flooring. The stainless-steel platform bed had a dark-brown fabric headboard attached to the wall. A faux-fur bedspread, made to look like rich sable, covered the bed. Ross couldn't deny himself, and kicked off his shoes to stretch out on bedspread. A snicker interrupted his daydream of having a blond or redhead cuddled up beside him.

"I thought you'd approve. Every Norman throwback should have fur on his bed. If you'd like, I'll show you what I did to the guest room."

Before following Nels, Ross got curious and lifted the corner of the bedspread to discover crimson sheets underneath. Perhaps he should try a brunette. The dark hair would go much better than a redhead with his new red sheets.

Ross caught up to Nels in the doorway of the guestroom and admitted to lagging behind for one last touch of the bedspread. If Nels had been a former teammate, his sardonic Mr. Spock-worthy lift of one eyebrow would've earned him a solid jab to the biceps.

"As you can see, I went with lighter colors in the guest room." Nels pointed to the white walls containing the faintest tinge of blue. To Ross, it resembled moonlight on snow and, upon closer inspection, it did sparkle a little. Another fur bedspread graced the guest bed but in a honey-blond shade. Nels had used the same honey oak flooring as in the kitchen.

Gesturing at the bed, Nels stated, "This is a new design for Danegeld. It's called a Nook bed. I went with aquamarine for the headboard. The wood dresser and nightstands are teak and, as you can see, they're a shade darker honey than the floor."

Overcome by curiosity, Ross peeked under the spread to discover ice-blue sheets. Not sure what this said about his renter, maybe Frost Prince, he followed Nels to the living room and came to a screeching halt. Nels had painted the walls a tea-with-cream color, and, holding pride of place on the newly installed oak flooring was a solitary rug in cream wool with a burnt orange tree in full bloom. It took his breath away.

When he could do nothing but gesture, Nels explained, "It's a depiction of *Yggdrasil*, the tree of life. I thought it would go well with whatever Danish designs you choose for this room. Once again, it's an exclusive Danegeld design. I got the store to lend it so you can see if you like it. You'll get a good discount if you decide to keep it, but it will have a significant impact on your wallet. I'll send it back if you find it too expensive."

"Not on your life, I'm keeping it. You did a magnificent job while I was away. I really appreciated you keeping me up-to-date by text and photos. So, what's next?"

"My least favorite part of decorating, window treatments, but I have a suggestion for avoiding having to install curtain rods." He smiled. "Or, we could start on your personal study, I think there's a stellar wooden mantle under those thirty coats of paint, and we could surround the fireplace itself with hand-painted tiles."

Ross startled a grunt from Nels when he dropped
to the rug and pulled the Dane down to sit with him.
"As much as I would like to start on my man cave, I
think we need to talk window treatments. The sheets
now decorating the windows for privacy don't do
justice to this beautiful rug. What's your suggestion for
avoiding fussy curtains? I gotta tell you, I don't care
for tacky plastic blinds, either."

"While you were out of town, I discovered a store
specializing in unusual window treatments. They have
panels you can raise or lower by remote control. They
are fabric-covered, and you can have them match the
wall color. They're designed to fit on the inside of the
window with no gaps. I brought the brochures home
for you to study. I've already measured all the
windows, so all you need to do is pick a contrasting
color or match the walls."

"Sometimes your efficiency scares the bejeezus
out of me, Nels, but I do appreciate it. Yeah, let's run
with it. I'm guessing the automatic blinds don't come
cheap, so let's hope I get another client with an
expensive problem to solve real soon."

Nels bumped shoulders with him. "I've already got
my fingers crossed. Well, I'm off to the bookstore. I've

got my key in case you go out as well."

With the guided tour concluded, Ross became aware Nels had indeed dressed for going out. The woodsy scent of aftershave should've been the first clue. Remembering his original intention to shower, Ross stood up and offered a hand up to his renter. "No problem. I haven't decided what I'll do this evening except not work." He'd almost added, maybe I'll catch up on some TV, but stifled it before the lame excuse for a single man's Friday night could be uttered.

\*\*\*

Nels ordered a triple espresso from the Jamaican barista. He flirted with her as she filled his order because he loved hearing the lilting Caribbean accent. Maybe he'd head on down to the islands when Ross's renovation project ended.

Seated at a table, he glanced at the index to the book he'd purchased at the bookstore next door and couldn't help thinking of Ross. The book's theme centered on the battle of Hastings, after all.

One word in the index caught his eye, *Danegeld*, and he thumbed to the correct chapter to read what the author had to say about his Danish ancestors. Nels grinned when the book told him he'd be able to lord it over Roslin de Lassy, but the humorous thought didn't quite squelch the disquiet he'd brought into the coffee shop with him.

He'd turn thirty in a short while and assume control of Danegeld. Rather than infuse him with eagerness to grasp the power, the thought depressed him. He wished he'd come to the States a year earlier. Maybe then he'd have had his fill of interacting with the exuberant Americans. Being rich didn't mean you couldn't envy the common man, and he found he did.

He admired the Americans for their openness and their affection. If an American thought something funny, they laughed full out. If they wanted to buy you a drink, they did so with no expectations of reciprocity. Unlike his own family, they touched each other constantly, from hugs to punches on the arm, and arms thrown over shoulders, or big smacking kisses without the least bit of embarrassment. Even if the gesture took place in public.

His grandfather had been the sole family member to understand his rebellious spirit, but even he'd saddled him with sober maturity by leaving him Danegeld. At least he'd been given him a brief respite from familial duty.

And, truth be told, he did want to settle down and work to make his company a success, but the thought of being shackled to a polite, reserved woman, one his parents would work hard to assure met their dull, constricted, social standards, left him wanting to bang his head on the table top.

Telling himself to suck it up, because sitting in a coffee shop and whining wouldn't delay the inevitable didn't leave him feeling any better. Maybe he was edgy for a reason. He hadn't gotten any in months. Maybe he needed to blow off a little sexual steam and sand down his sharp edges?

Snorting at his skill in self-diagnosis, Nels glanced out the front window and discovered the sun setting. Well aware of the condom in his wallet, he saw no reason not to find a bar and end his self-enforced abstinence. Perhaps a red head this time? Disposing of his empty cup, Nels walked out of the shop and straight into a group of men loitering on the sidewalk.

*** 

After his shower, Ross wandered into his new kitchen and ran his hand over his countertops. Maybe he'd fix himself a light dinner... or maybe not. He discovered nothing in his new refrigerator but bottled water and a six-pack minus two bottles. Guess I'm dining out this evening, he thought, but he didn't want to eat alone. Ross went straight to the desk in his unfinished study to search for the number he'd copied from his computer. When he found it, Ross wished he'd remembered to bring one of the cold beers in with him. He could've used a little liquid courage at the moment. *Okay, if it gets to three rings without an answer, I'm hanging up.*

The pick up on the second ring had him stuttering like a teenager. "H-hi, my name's Ross, and since you gave me your number on our last email exchange, I wondered if you might be free for dinner this evening. You are? Um, okay. Do you like Lebanese food? Yeah, I know the place. How about I meet you there at seven o'clock? Yes, I have dark-brown, short hair, and I'll be wearing a white shirt and red tie. See you there."

Ross hung up and went back to his room to change out of his jeans into something more date-worthy. Maybe his inspired choice of a red tie would pan out and he'd get to christen his new sheets this evening, and with a brunette no less.

As good luck omens went, the red tie proved to be a complete bust. His date turned out to be a groupie, a

51

special forces groupie. A few years ago, Ross might not have minded, and might even have been the first one between the sheets, but now he didn't want to be anyone's trophy fuck.

Against his better judgment, he'd clicked on to the sign up page for one of those Mates-R-Us web sites and had gotten a few hits, but from the tone of most of the emails he received, he'd been reluctant to connect. This one seemed to have a few intelligent brain cells, until he discovered the total narcissistic self-involvement, and obvious interest in banging a Green Beret. It appeared to him most of the people who signed up for the site wanted sex without commitment, a real wham, bam, and thank you ma'am buffet.

If he could've managed it physically, he would've kicked himself in the ass. First for having picked up the phone tonight, and yet again, for the make-out session afterward. He'd had to abort. His self-respect wouldn't let him go any farther. He returned home and stretched out on his fur bedspread by midnight, wondering if he'd ever find the one person who'd complete him.

It did nothing for his ego when he returned to find Nels's Ducati still missing from the driveway. At least the man had the decency not to drag his hookups back here. He didn't want to have to put on underwear or a robe in the morning to walk to the kitchen of his own house for his first cup of coffee.

Ross rolled over and turned off the light with a final thought for the disappointing evening. Maybe Mr. Prinz was right—being alone was better than being with someone totally wrong for him.

Well screw it. If it happened, it would happen when it happened, and he vowed to stop trying to make it happen. Perhaps he should ask for divine intervention. He stifled a laugh at his own expense. He needed to re-read the de Lassy genealogy chart because, given his dating record, there had to be a self-flagellating monk somewhere in the line. Oh, wait, that would be him, and, this time, Ross laughed aloud at the rude up and down gesture he made with his hand.

In the meantime, he would take out his frustrations with his MMA workout partner, Tomodashi-san, the little oriental sadist who delighted in punching, gouging, and kicking him into a pulp. It would effectively send his libido whimpering back to a neutral corner.

Bleary-eyed and unshaven, Ross plugged his percolator in at the ungodly hour of seven a. m.

Saturday morning. When the smell of fresh-brewed coffee didn't attract his renter, Ross ventured across the hallway and saw the guestroom door open. The bed hadn't been slept in. *Great, at least someone in the house got his rocks off.* Ross winced at his own crudity, went back to pour himself a cup of coffee, and took it with him back to his bedroom. A long bike ride in the country sounded like as a good idea. He would've asked Nels to ride along, but the man might still be engaged in riding of another sort.

The open road, and the purchase of a World War I knuckle-bow knife to add to his collection, spread some balm on his bad mood. He found Nels still in the missing category when he returned in late afternoon, but he forgot to be jealous as he switched his bike for his SUV to go shopping for food to stock the pantry and refrigerator.

The bill for all his purchases put him into another funk. Well at least he'd be able to cook his own damned meal, and if Nels showed up by the time he took it out of the oven, he'd be welcome to partake.

Ross spent Sunday filing case files and doing bookkeeping, an exercise he compared to the pain of having a root canal. When dinner time rolled around again, and still no Nels, Ross started to become concerned but reasoned a six-foot Dane didn't need a babysitter. Hell, if he possessed Nels's chick-magnet handsomeness, he wouldn't return until the wee hours of Monday morning, either.

Ross failed to come up with any explanation for why Nels was still MIA on Monday afternoon. They were supposed to visit the window shop so he could see how the things worked by remote control. Nels would never miss an appointment without calling, and the investigator in him screamed something was rotten in Denmark. Ross recalled Nels saying he intended to check out the local bookshop, so he'd start his search there.

Ross parked and studied the front of the coffee shop just across a narrow alley from a bookstore specializing in military history. He'd frequented the place himself once or twice, and had taken his purchases into the coffee shop to read away an hour or two. The location had slipped since his last visit. Gangs had decorated the storefront windows with graffiti and a few bullet holes in their pursuit of territory. Nels's Ducati parked out front increased his worry

Approaching the counter, Ross ordered a triple shot espresso and chatted up the Jamaican barista.

"Oh yeah, I know Mr. Nels. Mmm, mmm, mmm,

that man is fine. So polite, and with his English accent, he melts the fudge right off my brownies. He came in here late Friday afternoon, ordered the same thing you did, and spent a couple of hours reading a book. Next time I saw him, he'd gone outside and was talking to a group of either Latino or Arabic men who have been hanging around outside. I had a customer place an order right then, and by the time I checked again, he'd left."

Ross tipped well for the information and coffee and went outside. He took a right into the narrow, dark alley between the coffee shop and the bookstore. Removing a small Maglite from his pocket, he flashed it from side to side as he walked its length and came to a book lying, spine-broken and soiled, in the detritus of the alley. When he picked it up, a business card fell out. His. Nels had been using it as a bookmark, because a bibliophile such as himself never dog-eared a page. Ross's stomach clenched when he turned it over to discover *The Battle of Hastings* emblazoned on the cover and blood on the flyleaf. A few steps farther, he found Nels's cell phone and wallet with credit cards still in it, but no cash. He'd already espied the multiple footprints in a moving, scuffing pattern, but now he could add a set of long marks in the middle of them, like someone had gone limp and been dragged. The alley came out on a street where a car could pull up and take away whoever had made those marks in the debris. From the visible signs, and the barista's mention of a group of loitering men, Ross began to think Nels might not have left the area willingly.

Ross returned home to gather his thoughts. Fetching a yellow legal pad, he poured a glass of Scotch and started a list of things he knew about his renter. Nels exuded intelligence, but he wasn't in your face about it. The only books he'd seen Nels bring into the house were history or art books. Maybe it was the Dane in him, but he seemed more reserved than the average twentysomething, single American guy, so he didn't think Nels was a womanizer. There hadn't been many nights he hadn't made it home by the end of the evening, so chances were his disappearance wasn't based on a married woman's schedule. Besides, his gut told him Nels was too honorable to sneak around with a married woman.

Gambling was a no go as well. Nels had money to spare, but while generous with it, never spent in excess. So being roughed up for non-payment of vig was out. Even if he had run up a large debt, whoever came to collect would've only roughed him up as incentive to get the money together, not made him disappear. Ross speculated about a possible drug problem, but his eyes were always crystal clear and his hands rock steady when using tools.

The next page on the pad he devoted to things that might've made Nels a target. Lack of street smarts topped the list, and a true pang of guilt hit him for not offering to teach the man a few basics. Half the time, Nels was totally oblivious to who shared the street with him, or that he turned heads when he passed people.

For the first time Ross felt a guy could perhaps be too handsome for his own good. Nels's lack of attention to who occupied his space had probably made it really easy for that group of men to jump him and drag him into that alley.

From Nels's interest in his own pocket knife, Ross knew the man didn't carry one, especially not one good for doing something more than paring nails, for Christ's sake. Well, if this situation had a positive resolution, Nels would get some self-defense training, whether he wanted it or not. Ross snorted in disgust at the too-little too-late thought. Had they tried snatching him, there would've been unconscious and bleeding bodies in front of the coffee shop.

A poisonous puffball of a thought suddenly blossomed in his mind at the end of his list-making. It had him slamming his empty glass back on the table and thumbing through his personal contacts on his phone. He hoped like hell he was way off base, but he needed to bounce it off an area expert, one Walt Giordano of the Alexandria police force.

Ross began to breathe a little easier when he heard Walt bark into the phone, "Giordano here," but his tension returned with Walt's questions, after he explained the reason for his call.

"What was the address of this coffee shop?" When Ross explained what he knew, the man groaned. "Okay, give me a description of your friend."

"Well, he's about twenty-eight or nine, about six foot two, and has white-blond hair and very light-blue eyes. He's not a US citizen. He's Danish, but speaks with an English accent."

"Any tattoos or distinguishing marks?"

"I've seen him with his shirt off, but I didn't notice any. He's been renting a room from me and helping me restore my townhouse. He's a good worker, and punctual to a fault, but he went out Friday night and he hasn't called at all over the weekend. I found his cell phone and wallet in that alley."

"Would you say your friend is handsome?"

Ross visualized Nels as he answered. "Yeah, I've seen him turn a few heads on women at Home Depot when we've gone in for supplies. The man wouldn't have any trouble getting a date. He's a tennis player and swimmer, so he's pretty fit, but he dresses kind of quirky, like a nerd. He wears hand-knotted bow ties for God's sake but drives a classic Ducati, which is still parked in front of the coffee shop."

Walt sighed in a resigned manner. "I don't want to scare you, Ross, but a Latino criminal gang is operating in that area, and they've managed to achieve a certain notoriety. They don't deal so much in drugs as in prostitution, specifically the male sex-slave trade. They've carved out a real niche for themselves by taking orders for specific features. If your friend has the pale-blond hair, blue eyes, and the athletic body you've just described, they could've snatched him to fill a particular order."

"Isn't he a little too old for that?"

"Umm, I'd like to say yes, but who the hell knows what turns some people's cranks. I think you might want to contact the FBI on this because blond males are a favorite order for certain Middle Eastern deviants. I have a contact there, if you need one."

Ross felt a sharp jab straight to his solar plexus at Walt's last revelation. "No thanks, Walt. I have my own sources. Thanks for your help. If you do find anything at all, here's my cell phone number. And before you suggest it, I'm not going to sit back and let others do all the work. I can turn up more leads by getting into places where uniforms aren't welcome."

"As long as you're not thinking of turning vigilante, I'll overlook your last remark. If I find out anything at all about your friend I'll be in touch."

By the time Ross arranged to have Nels's bike towed back to his place, re-scouted the neighborhood for anything he might've missed, grabbed a dinner he never tasted, and returned to his house, it was very late. He needed to go through Nels's room to see if could find any clue to lead him in a more promising direction. He hoped there would be, as it had to be a better situation than the one his handyman might be in now.

A search of the guest room closet told him Nels hadn't lied. He didn't have a lot in the way of clothes, just a few pair of jeans, button down and T-shirts, a tweed sports coat, tennis whites, sneakers. The dresser contained a dozen pair of socks in white and black, and multiple pairs of white underwear. Nels wore boxer-briefs like himself.

At his last sight of the Dane, he'd been wearing a pair of jeans, T-shirt, Wellington boots, and his leather jacket. There were no clues to be found amidst the shaving cream, toothpaste, toothbrush, comb, and hair brush, and the bottle of aftershave. The single bottle of aspirin squelched the idea of any drug addiction. The man was disgustingly healthy. Ross replaced the box of condoms, the same brand he used, he'd found in the nightstand next to the bed. At least the man practiced safe sex.

Disappointed at the lack of information to guide his search, Ross was about to call it quits for the evening when he remembered telling Nels he could use the third floor as his art studio. He had no idea what a box of paints and an easel could tell him, but he'd search the studio, all the same.

As it turned out, he did discover Nels had fantastic talent, as he studied the charcoal outline on the canvas he'd placed on the easel. It suggested a forest scene, but Nels hadn't gotten very far with it.

The sketch pad tossed on the floor drew his attention next, and he sat down on the canvas drop cloth Nels used to protect the floor from paint splatters. Upon opening the book, Ross saw his renter possessed the skill to be one hell of a portrait painter. He should've been devoting most of his attention to painting rather than taking odd jobs or running a furniture company. Hell, he'd buy any one of the drawings, especially if Nels executed them in oil or watercolor.

The last drawing made him forget to breathe. Nels had drawn Ross as a Norman knight. The scene had the suggestion of castle walls in the background, with the knight's great warhorse unsaddled and cropping grass. The saddle, helm, chainmail, and surcoat were strewn on the ground, with the great sword, with its plain, cross-shaped hilt driven, point down, into the grass. It gave him the impression the knight deliberately left it ready to hand in case he needed to fend off enemies.

A little embarrassed at seeing a representation of himself, Ross forced himself to note the bowl cut of the knight's hair, his own stark visage, and that he'd been drawn coming out of a pond, as if he'd stopped to wash off a day of hard training.

Nels had even drawn a puckered scar of a healed wound on his shoulder. While his had been made by a bullet, an arrow or sword point might've left a similar mark on the knight. Nels drew the musculature and proportions of the body in such detail he could almost see the water beading on the knight's body as he walked from the pond.

If Nels ever thought of selling this sketch to a gallery, he'd bankrupt himself before he let it leave his house. No way did he want anyone gawking at a portrait of himself *au naturel*. He did discover one, teensy historical inaccuracy in the sketch, and resolved to tease the Oxford historian the next time they spoke.

The thought he might never see Nels again sent him flying downstairs. With no clues to contradict Walt's theory on why Nels had been taken, he needed some serious help if he ever expected to speak with him again.

C'mon, c'mon, pick up your damned phone, Ross muttered as he counted the sixth ring.

"Whoever this is better have a good goddamn reason for calling my private number at this time of night," hissed an irritated Bronx-accented voice.

"Bernie, its Ross de Lassy."

"Dawg? Look man, as much as I'd love to chat about what great times we had in ACE, I'm a little busy having a great time of my own right now, if you catch my drift. Call me in the morning, and we'll take a trip down memory lane together."

"Sorry, Bernie, no can do. I think I have a situation here, and it's time sensitive. Do you know of any trafficking rings operating in the Alexandria area?"

"Give me a second, Lassie. I need to get to my, um, other office."

Ross heard the murmurings of an apology to whichever woman occupied Bernie's bed, and then silence until Bernie asked his own question.

"Are we talking drug trafficking or people trafficking?"

"People."

"Is the woman in question young, blond, and attractive, or is it a child?"

"Uh, the man in question is in his mid to late twenties, tall, blond, and handsome in a Danish Viking sort of way."

"Shit, Dawg, wish I could say his being an adult male would exclude him, but we've had our eyes on a ring. They go by the name *Sangritos* or Little Bloods because they're mixed race, Afro-American and Hispanic. They're specialists and stick to the sex trade, and they've been selecting males based on hair color or body build. They make their selections off a computer-generated shopping list, and word has it, the purchasers, who're rolling in oil, can afford their exorbitant finder's fees. So far it's been pre-pubescent or teen-age males, but if the guy is as handsome as you say he is, he'd be a definite item of interest."

Ross began to swear under his breath but stopped when Bernie continued speaking.

"We haven't been able to catch them in the act yet, but we're getting closer. We do know they've been making pickups in your general area and putting them up for sale at a location somewhere in the Baltimore Inner Harbor vicinity. I wish to God we could find the place and bust this ring wide open. We lost a college kid a month ago, and we think they nabbed an eight-year-old boy last week.

"Do you have anything I can use to close them down?"

Ross pinched the bridge of his nose to relieve some of the pounding headache he'd developed while Bernie briefed him. "If these guys are the ones who took my...." Ross hesitated, he'd almost said renter, but Nels had become more than a renter. He'd become a friend. "Who took my friend. There were three of them, and they appeared to be from the Latino gang who moved into the Old Town, Alexandria, area. There didn't appear to be a public struggle, but I found footprints and drag marks in an alley next to the abduction site."

"I'd bet they gave him a quick injection of ketamine. It would render him meek and mild in an instant. When did this happen?"

"Near as I can figure, around dusk on Friday. I'd been out of town, and he agreed to accompany me to an appointment on Monday to see about installing remote control blinds, but when he didn't show up for breakfast for the third morning in a row, I began to reassess the idea he'd been doing the bump and grind all weekend.

"Maybe your friend just wanted a long weekend off."

"Nels, would never ditch work, or not call if something had come up to keep him away. I checked out his favorite haunts, and a barista at the local coffee shop said she'd seen him talking to some dark-skinned guys right after he left the coffee shop.

"Since, as you say, you haven't known him all that long, he might've met up with some friends of his."

"I don't think these were friends, Bernie. A contact of mine in the Alexandria police force told me a Latino gang is operating in the area, and is making a bad name for themselves."

Bernie blew out an audible sigh. "Yep, that coffee shop is in Sangrito territory, and they are bad operators. If they took him Friday last, he's probably still in Baltimore. Thanks to modern technology and conference calling, he'll be put up for auction, and the bidding will all be done by computer. The pervs who bid will be able to see what they're bidding on, but your guy will be drugged to the gills. At least the Sangritos won't abuse him in any way. That's the prerogative of whoever buys him."

Ross's gut clenched. "Bernie, do you have even a small clue as to where they might be keeping him while they hold this auction?"

"I'd say it's close to Baltimore Washington International Airport. Once the merchandise is purchased, they transport them via private charter. This gang moves merchandise almost as efficiently as FedEx. I'm saying plane, but it could be a freighter or container ship. The port of Norfolk is close."

"I'm a one-man operation, Bernie. It will be next to impossible to cover much ground searching for Nels in a sea of cargo containers."

"I wish I could offer you some hope, Lassie, but I'm afraid your friend will spend the rest of his life as a sex slave, or, if they can't break him, they'll kill him and bury him under a sand dune."

Ross had more or less expected Bernie's bad news, but hearing it in plain English left cold sweat on his forehead. "Thanks for the info, even if it wasn't what I wanted to hear. As you know, I'm pretty good at finding lost things. When I find Nels, I'll be sure he gives you enough information to plow this ring six feet under."

Ross tried to call it a night to clear his mind and consider his next moves, but it proved to be impossible. Instead, he found himself making an omelet at four in the morning. Cooking relaxed him, and since he missed a few meals yesterday, his growling stomach made it hard for him to concentrate. He needed help, but first he needed some protein to get the brain cells firing on all cylinders.

The aha moment came with the last bite of western omelet. Recalling the details of his last client's dossier, the one whose wife had been selling herself for cocaine, Ross cleaned up the kitchen and headed for a shower. Waiting for the hours to pass until he could call the man without rousting him from his bed made Ross mental, but at least he now had freshly washed and dried clothes as proof he'd put the waiting to good use.

When Elmer Prinz picked up his phone on the first ring, Ross didn't beat around the bush. The man preferred things direct and he wouldn't disappoint him.

"I have a favor to ask, Mr. Prinz. Do you have any contacts in the BWI private jet arena? I need to have access to who comes in and out of there, especially if they're from the Middle East."

"Yeah, I do, as a matter of fact. Our corporate jet flies out of there. Do you need to be there, or is access to the computers all you need? I wanna tell you, you saved my company and my bank account. My soon-to-be ex is drying out in New York, and my attorney has given her a more-than-generous settlement. She's agreed to go without a fuss. So, whatever you need, you've got. How soon do you need this to happen?"

"Now would be a good time. I'm not going to lie to you. This is a time-sensitive, operation."

"Got it. Give me a minute, and I'll call you back."

Elmer Prinz proved to be well worth the money he made as a corporate CEO. Blending in with the shift change, Ross wore a set of aviation mechanic overalls, and appeared to know what he had to fix on the airplane engine in front of him, but he wouldn't touch anything other than to wipe his greasy hands on a rag.

His attention was on a recent arrival from Saudi Arabia. A quick computer check of the tail number confirmed the owner as Prince al-Harbi.

Ross remained stationary as the two men listed on the manifest disembarked. They wore the traditional *thawbs*, *shumaghs*, *igals* and *mishlas* of Saudi men. From his former career, he could tell both had personal security all but stamped on the front of their *shumaghs* or head covers.

The pilot and copilot appeared to be Westerners, and they'd stayed behind long enough to get the plane ready for departure, which, Ross verified, had been scheduled for takeoff in the bare minimum of time needed for pilot rest.

Ross's gut told him this plane was a good possibility. The geographic region matched up, the airport lined up as well, and the quick turnaround time made him think of quick getaways. If someone had purchased Nels within the last few days, they'd want to get him the hell out of the country as soon as possible.

Ross wished he could clone himself, or had another partner, because he couldn't cover both airport and port, so he put all his chips on the plane, reasoning whoever purchased Nels wouldn't want to wait for the month a ship would take to reach Jeddah from Norfolk before he could enjoy his new toy.

The next afternoon, Ross pretended to sweep the hangar floor as he watched the pilot and copilot walk toward their plane. He now knew Prince al-Harbi to be a distant relative of the current Saudi king, and the plane was a sweet Gulfstream G650.

Keeping his eyes fixed on the small mound of dust he'd collected, Ross had a cynical thought. If Nels left the United States aboard al-Harbi's jet, he'd be going in style.

He had the entire hangar floor spotless by time the pilots completed the pre-flight inspection and waited aboard for the return of the two security thugs.

The jet's two passengers weren't alone when they showed up. They had another man supported between them, and he staggered as if drunk or drugged. Ross used the cover of a wheeled baggage carriage to move closer, and when the wind blew through the open hangar door, it lifted the red and white embroidered *shumagh* away from the unknown man's face, and he caught a silver gilt glint from the man's beard. Even with a beard, Ross recognized Nels.

Ross knew where the plane would land, although he didn't know to whom Nels would be taken once it landed, but he would bet his left nut the owner of the plane he had under surveillance was not involved in this.

Al-Harbi was a trusted liaison between the ruling family and the OPEC Board, and if he did have a perverted kink for young men, he'd managed to keep it deeply hidden for a very long time. But the prince had a very large family, and Ross would wager there was a twisted apple or two hanging from the lower branches.

Thanks to the computer access Elmer Prinz arranged for him, he also had the names of the two security guys sent to pick up the package. Local law enforcement couldn't touch a hair on the head of anyone in that plane, due to Prince al-Harbi's diplomatic immunity, so Ross didn't attempt to stop the plane from leaving, just stripped off his overalls and left the hangar.

He didn't work for anyone there, punch a time clock, or collect a salary, so no one would miss him. As a courtesy to Mr. Prinz, he would destroy the fake ID badge allowing him access to the facility. Right now he needed his passport and go bag. He'd buy anything else he needed through his connections at the American embassy in Riyadh. The station chief of a three-letter agency there was a personal friend.

# Chapter Six

Nels woke with a raging headache and a mouth so dry he thought he'd been munching on cotton balls while he slept. He raised his head to study his whereabouts, and discovered he lay in a huge, circular bed, curled around a beautiful redhead. For the life of him, he couldn't remember how he got to wherever this was. Squeezing his eyes shut to aid his memory made the bed spin, but he still couldn't recall anything after he left the coffee shop to head back to Ross's house, and, God help him, he didn't remember receiving a bedroom invitation. He began to panic this might be a symptom of permanent loss of his eidetic memory.

Nels forced his eyes to open wide before the spinning sensation made him empty the bile from his stomach. Attracted by the unusual color of the hair cascading down the woman's back, Nels tried to recall where he might've met her, and once again drew a blank. Damn, tactile sense alone told him he lay spooned against her, with his nude hip and thigh snugged into the woman's ass, and he couldn't remember her name. Mortifying in the extreme.

To assist his memory, Nels stole a lock of the unusual colored tresses, and discovered it to be the texture of pure silk. It reminded him of the rose-gold jewelry his mother favored. He took a moment to admire the woman's luxuriant hair cascading past her delicious round ass.

The artist in Nels began positioning his, unidentified as of yet, model in his mind for a portrait. Beautiful wavy hair, nice firm ass, well-shaped legs with nice musculature, and slender wrists banded by gold bracelets studded with emeralds. Upon closer inspection he found the fingers, long and tapered, didn't match up with the hands. The hands were too mannish, and the sleeping beauty's feet gave him the same vibe. He must've made a tsk of disapproval, for his model turned to face him in her sleep, and what he saw launched him off the bed. What his bed partner lacked in breasts, she made up for in penis and testicles.

Nels's sudden movement woke the man whom Nels estimated to be in his late teens. "God in heaven, where the hell am I, and how did I get here?" Nels didn't realize he'd given voice to the thought until the boy answered his questions.

"Good morning, Templar. You're in Saudi Arabia. As to where in Saudi Arabia, I can't say, because I don't know. How did you get here? I'd say someone kidnapped and drugged you. I hope you last longer than my last roommate, I get bored talking to myself. Oh, forgive my rudeness for not introducing myself. My name's Wren, and I'm to be your teacher."

"Why do you call me Templar? My name is—"

The self-named Wren jumped out of bed and put his hand over Nels's lips.

"Shhh, there are no names but the names our master has given us. Your name is Templar, and my name is Wren, like the little bird. Our master may have another name, but we will never address him as anything other than Master."

The strain in the boy's voice spoke of fear, so Nels chose to pursue the other part of Wren's sentence and removed Wren's hand from his mouth. "What are you supposed to teach me?"

His question brought Wren chest-to-chest with him, and Nels flinched when Wren cupped his face.

"Why I'm to teach you how to please our master in bed."

Nels had frozen at the full body contact, so Wren's kiss took him by surprise. So gentle and fleeting a kiss, he could almost imagine it'd never happened. Wren jumped back when he jerked his head away.

"See? Not so bad for a first lesson. At least you're too old to cry. My former roommate did nothing but for days on end. I think he must've made himself ill, for one day he answered the master's summons and never returned. I hope he's happier wherever he is now."

The young man spoke in English, but Nels couldn't connect his words with anything that made sense. Aside from language, something else disturbed him. Wren seemed too naive for his physique, and he asked, "How old are you, Wren?"

Wren laughed and jangled his bracelets. "I was brought here when I was eleven and given these emerald rings to match the color of my eyes. The next year, and for each year after, I got one bracelet as a gift. I have three bracelets on my left wrist and three on my right, so that makes me eighteen. I see our Master has given you aquamarines to match your eyes. You really have very pretty eyes, Templar."

Wren's accounting of his age by jewelry made Nels aware of Wren's gem-studded nipple and navel rings and wrist bracelets. But when the boy pointed to him and mentioned aquamarines, he realized the source of

77

the stinging sensation in his own chest. Looking down the length of his body made him gasp when he discovered he'd been similarly adorned, to include, judging by the sting, one on the underside of his penis. His mortification increased when he noted his entire body had been waxed, oiled and, if his face mirrored Wren's, he was wearing a fine line of kohl around each eye.

Nels's entire body began to tremble. So much so, he didn't protest when Wren reached up and ran his hand over his cheek.

He remained silent and miserable when Wren cocked his head and studied him.

"I guess our master likes your beard because he's left it on. It does make you look like a Knight Templar. I read about them in one of my history books. If you please him, our master can be very generous. I have but to write what I want on a piece of paper and the Oompa Loompas collect it, and it magically appears a few days later."

At the mention of the strange sounding name, Nels collapsed back onto the bed, and jumped out of the way when Wren followed as well. "What in the hell are Oompa Loompas?"

"Oh, I'm being silly. They aren't Oompa Loompas

like the ones in the movie, *Willy Wonka and the Chocolate Factory*. It's a name I gave the men who come in to clean this room and restock the refrigerator or bring the prepared meals. I had to make a name up because they never speak to me.

Nels tried to speak, but only a croak came out.

"Are you thirsty, Templar? I can offer you a glass of juice or bottled water or even a Coca Cola. Sorry, we aren't permitted alcoholic beverages. There is always fresh fruit to snack on if you're hungry."

As he asked for bottled water, Nels prayed he'd regain his senses and find this had all been a bizarre hallucination. When he hesitated to take it from Wren's hand, the boy reassured him.

"Go ahead, it isn't drugged. You're the master's property, so you will be well cared for. The Oompas won't drug you except on the days you need to be groomed."

"Groomed?" Nels sputtered. "I'm capable of washing myself, brushing my teeth, and combing my hair. I can even shave myself, if given a razor."

He didn't think his declaration was funny at all, but Wren laughed with such mirth he rolled right off the bed.

"I didn't mean that kind of grooming. Trust me,

you'll appreciate not having all of your senses when they wax your body. Once they didn't give me a large enough dose, and I can assure you, having the hair stripped off your balls and anus is quite painful."

Nels cringed inwardly. The boy either had no shame or no verbal filter. He managed to stop his hand before he cupped himself at Wren's description of the process. Wren continued enumerating the household rules.

"And as for a razor, you won't get one. Nothing is permitted in this room that can cut or stab or cause bodily injury. All of our meals will be eaten with our fingers or plastic utensils, which are counted and collected after every meal.

"If your hair or beard need trimming, the Oompa Loompas will see to it, but they won't drug you for that. Our Master likes my hair long so it has never been cut, except the ends to make it healthy. I braid it after I wash it so it dries with waves in it."

If he got the chance to play teacher, the first lesson Nels would give Wren would be how to erect a filter between first thought and verbalization, but for now he'd explore the room and see how he could escape.

The one, screened window in the room drew him

like a dowsing rod found water. It was low enough and wide enough to accommodate his body, but the screen was solid metal and very ornate. He could barely make out shapes through the small pin holes. The only function the window served was to let air in to be circulated by the overhead fan.

When he pushed against the screen, it didn't budge. Since they weren't to be given any kind of pointed utensil, Nels couldn't see a way of removing it. Maybe he'd ask the Oompa Loompas for a cannon.

Giving the window up as a lost cause for the moment, Nels studied the rest of the room, and found it furnished like something out of a modern Arabian Nights tale. It contained a large, round bed covered in bright sheets, and a wide chaise lounge. Appliances included a refrigerator and microwave, but no stove.

His roving eyes stopped at an arched doorway, and, when he entered it, he discovered a huge marble bathroom with a glassed-in shower stall, and a free-standing tub the size of a small swimming pool. A toilet, bidet, urinal, and a double sink, with all the wall fixtures in gold-plate, completed the bathroom. Whoever the master was, he wasn't poor.

Nels noted the sneer on his face in the gilt-edged mirror. It confirmed what he'd suspected. He'd been made to resemble a cross between a Knight Templar and a cast extra for a low-budget porn flick.

Returning to the main room, Nels realized what he'd been searching for—clothes. He hadn't found any clothes in the main room, and the bathroom did contain towels, but none large enough to use as decent covering.

"Wren, where are our clothes?"

Wren, who'd stretched out on his stomach on the bed, raised his eyes from the book he'd been reading. "We don't have any. We're given white cotton pants when our master wants to see us, or when we are taken to the walled garden so the Oompas can clean our room. We don't need clothes, Templar. The blankets on the bed will keep us warm at night, and it gets too hot during the day to even want them."

What Wren said next shook him to the soles of his feet.

"Our master likes to see our bodies, so we're never to cover up unless it's nighttime."

When the boy flicked his eyes toward the ceiling, Nels realized the room contained closed-circuit cameras. Now, Wren's quick hushing of him when he tried to say his name made sense.

He wanted to stare into the camera and say fuck

you, but the irony of it made him lose the urge. Tired and defeated for the moment, Nels stretched out on the bed and closed his eyes. He didn't even protest when Wren moved up to sit behind him and stroked his hair.

"I'm glad you're not crying, Templar. If the other boy, who cried all the time, had let me, I would've soothed him. I'm good at giving massages. See?, Isn't having your hair and scalp rubbed making you relax? I promise not to touch anywhere else...for now. I want us to be friends. I've been lonely without someone to talk to, and even though I like to read and listen to music, having another person in the room is better."

Wren hadn't exaggerated his massage skills. Nels could feel his eyes grow heavy and his muscles release the hard knots he'd been keeping them in. He'd reached mental overload, and so gave in to sleep.

Being taller and stronger than Wren, there wouldn't be a problem holding him off if he tried anything. He didn't think the boy would molest him in his sleep, because Wren sounded sincere about wanting a friend. But his détente would not extend to the boy's master. Let the fucker come into this room, and he'd find out how well a Templar fought.

# Chapter Seven

John Adams, distant relation to the second President of the United States, welcomed Ross into his private office in the American embassy. "Good to see you again, Lassie. I thought I heard through the grapevine you'd retired from the fast life, so I'm hoping this is you on vacation, and not you undercover and about to dump a whole shitload of trouble on my desk, like when you and your um, friends, visited me the last time."

"Yeah, Jack, I'm out of the service, but I can't say I won't be bringing some trouble along for this ride. Can I speak in here?"

"Do you mean like between two friends shooting the breeze, or like we need to take a walk in the open air?"

Ross glanced around the office and through the window to the swaying palms outside. "You know, it's a long plane ride from the States to here, and I could sure use a walk to stretch the kinks out."

Adams shook his head and rubbed the back of his neck. "I guess I have enough time before my next

C.L. Hadyn

meeting to get a little exercise. I wouldn't want to develop a gut from too much sitting. Come on, we can walk to a little café I know and grab some coffee."

Ross waited until they were alone on the street to begin. "I'm here because a friend of mine was grabbed off the street in Alexandria, Virginia, by a criminal gang specializing in the sex trade. I witnessed him being loaded aboard a Gulfstream G650 two days ago. The plane is registered to Prince al-Harbi, and it landed at King Khaled International. The names of the passengers on board are Abdullah Malik and Mohammed Fateen. I need to know who these men work for, and where they reside, because I'm pretty sure wherever they are, I'll find my friend."

"Now wait a minute, Lassie. You can't go running around like a one-man wrecking crew until you find where he's being kept."

"I'm not trying to be. That's why I came to you."

"You mentioned Prince al-Harbi, a Saudi royal, so your problem just became political rather than criminal. Sorry, but if Prince al-Harbi is in any way involved, your friend's situation has become exponentially more difficult."

"You were always good at seeing the big picture, Jack."

85

Jack snorted his disdain of the obvious flattery. "I'm assuming you want me to find out what I can, and I will, but you have to promise not to go in there shooting first and leaving me to clean up a, pardon the pun, royal mess after your departure."

Ross reined in his urge to ignore Jack's warning, and gave him what he wanted to hear. "Scout's honor, Jack. Get me the information and you'll never know I've been here."

John Adams tossed Ross a sour look. "Yeah, yeah. We both know I'm not doing this because we're such good friends, but because having a little leverage on people in high places can be profitable for the agency. I'm assuming your need to know has a short fuse."

Ross looked away and stared at nothing at all. "It's probably too late to spare my friend from being raped, or beaten severely if he resists, but the sooner the better. I'm afraid if he puts up too much resistance, he'll be killed, and they'll bury him somewhere I'll never find him."

"I'm aware of the urgency, de Lassy, but I'm going to have to go through channels on this."

Ross handed Adams a slip of paper. "I'm staying at the Intercontinental. Here's my room number and phone. I'll be playing innocent tourist in the meantime, but don't take too long, Jack, or I may have to start tipping over rocks myself."

"I wouldn't advise that, Lassie. I'll get you the info you need, but stay put until I do so. And it goes without saying I want to know exactly what you plan to do before you do it. I'm going to play nice with you, but you really don't want to see how mean I can be if you fuck me over on this."

Ross's lips twisted in a rueful smile. "Yeah, I'd heard that about you, Jack. I'll play nice. Since my friend wasn't exactly carrying his passport when they grabbed him, I'll need your help to get him out of the country without causing an international incident, so I'll stay on your good side."

After parting with Adams, Ross spent the rest of the day poolside, and dined on the terrace of the hotel's Al Bustan restaurant, which overlooked well-kept tropical gardens. If he'd been truly on vacation, he might have appreciated the international cuisine or the lush landscaping, but he couldn't keep from wondering what was happening to Nels. As he picked up the small cup of Arabic coffee to finish the meal, he made a vow he'd get the Dane back alive or there'd definitely be some bodies for Jack to clean up.

By the next morning, Ross already knew staring at

his room phone wouldn't make it ring, so he opted to play sightseer in the local souk. He bought himself a pair of gold cufflinks in the Zal market and then took a cab to Prince Sultan Boulevard to dine in the Arabic food court for lunch, but he couldn't make himself stay away from his phone a minute longer. It was with a great whoosh of relief he returned to his room to see the red message light blinking.

Keeping his words innocuous, Ross returned the call. "Hi, Jack, you called? I was out sightseeing. Riyadh has changed a bit since I was last here."

Jack played along. "Yes, I did call." "Hey, I'm sorry I had to cut our meeting short yesterday, but I'd like to make it up to you. How about you meet me at the same coffee shop, and I'll take you to a great restaurant I know. How does six o'clock sound?"

"Sounds perfect. See you at six." Ross hung up and went to wash off the dust of the souks. Knowing Jack's patrician tastes, it would be a five-star restaurant, but he'd spring for dinner. The man deserved to be wined and dined for such a quick turnaround time. He'd even wear his new gold cufflinks.

When they were seated across from one another at the luxury restaurant, Jack handed Ross a brochure.

"Here, I brought this for you, since you're interested in sightseeing."

Ross glanced at the brochure's cover and burst out, "Camel rides?"

Adams's eyes twinkled. "Well, yes, I think everyone should ride a camel at least once in their life, don't you? If you open the brochure, you'll find all the information you need to set up an excursion. Oh, and you'll also find the name of a shop where you can purchase whatever you'll need to make the ride enjoyable."

Ross tucked the brochure into his inside coat pocket without opening it. He knew Jack had placed the information he needed inside the brochure, but he wouldn't read it until he got back to his room.

The waiter arrived at their table to take their orders, and he and Jack spent the meal speaking of former acquaintances and former countries lived in. Anyone overhearing their conversation would've been bored to death.

The next morning, Ross rented a four-wheel drive vehicle and drove to the location he'd found in the brochure. It turned out to be a mud-walled compound in the middle of nowhere, owned by the son-in-law of Prince al-Harbi. The two men listed on the manifest of his plane worked for his son-in-law Farrid.

Meticulous to a fault, Jack had annotated the man had another residence closer to his father-in-law's, and surmised it housed Farrid's wife and children. Ross had to agree. He didn't think Farrid would chance having his predilections so close to the prince's scrutiny. The isolated compound was a sounder bet.

Parking his car on the side of the road, Ross moved closer to the walled dwelling on foot, an open map in his hands. If someone stopped him, he'd pretend to be lost and seeking directions.

His luck seemed to be holding when he spotted a weedy grove of palms on a rise offering a good view of the house and gardens. Making his way there, he sat down and removed a pair of miniature binoculars to study the residence.

Ross counted himself lucky to see no guards walking the perimeter, and breathed a sigh of relief when he didn't hear any barking dogs to alert the owner he had uninvited company.

People in this part of the world built walls around their residences and topped them with bits of broken glass and barbed wire. But unlike most compounds, here the wire had been turned to keep people in rather than thieves out.

A two-story tower at the far end drew his eye. While all of the windows on the ground floors had bars installed, he could still see through them, but an ornate metal screen covered the tower window and blocked any view of the interior. Ross would bet the property owner didn't want anyone to know what he kept there. But as anyone who'd ever done surveillance knew, the harder you tried to hide something, the more someone wanted to know what you were hiding.

Having seen enough for one day, Ross pocketed the binoculars and walked back to his vehicle. He'd return late this evening and set up his hiding place. He'd be bringing the equipment he'd need to verify Nels was inside the compound. He needed to be certain because if he went charging in there and discovered he had the wrong residence, Jack would roast his balls over a slow flame once the political shit storm settled down. Provided Jack still worked at the embassy in Riyadh, and hadn't reached retirement age, when he got out of whichever Saudi jail they threw him in.

\*\*\*

Nels woke up the next morning to find he'd been

placed into some sort of a warped *déjà vu* scenario. Once again, he found himself wrapped around a beautiful redhead, but this time he knew which sex. His unconscious body had sought out Wren for warmth or comfort, but he didn't intend to get too cozy. Trying to back away as surreptitiously as he could, Nels made it to the bathroom without waking his bedmate, but when he returned he found the boy up and combing out the braid he'd plaited his hair in before retiring the previous evening.

"Good morning, Templar. The Oompa Loompas will be bringing breakfast soon. I hope you like fresh fruit and juice, yogurt with flatbread, and olives in olive oil."

"As long as it comes with coffee, I don't care what they bring." When Wren's face fell, Nels asked, "Don't you drink coffee?"

"No. I prefer cardamom tea, but we can write them a note and have them bring coffee tomorrow, if they don't bring it today."

It seemed the mute Oompas read minds, for Nels spotted the copper coffee urn on the serving tray. It unnerved him to be sitting nude in a roomful of men, two of whom wouldn't meet his eyes as they straightened the bed linens, and a third who piled two of everything onto a plate before offering it to him with a wide grin and a wink.

Hunger got the better of his reservations, so Nels accepted the plate and poured a small cup of the strong Arabic coffee. *Yow!* The strong, thick brew would keep him wired for the rest of the day. Feeling the need to break the silence as well as his fast, Nels asked, "So what's the schedule around here, Wren? I'm assuming you get meals at certain times."

Wren swallowed and wiped his mouth on a linen napkin before answering. "Oh yes. We get breakfast two hours after sunrise and lunch around noon. The lunch meal is the heaviest, and then we get a smaller meal sometime around seven. I'm really just guessing at the times, since there are no clocks in here, but the angles of the sun seem to suggest those times.

"We'll be taken to the garden for sun and exercise around ten while the Oompa Loompas finish cleaning this room, and then we're free to do what we want until our master wants to see us. I usually read or watch a movie or listen to music, but now I can teach you.

"If there is anything you want, we'll write it down and leave it on the bed before we go to the garden this morning, and before you ask for it, Internet access,

93

cable television, fax, or phone will never be
permitted."

If he couldn't have those, what he wanted was the
key to the door, some clothes, a car, and a plane ticket
out of here. However, he didn't think the Oompas
would carry that list to their master. Nels settled for
the attainable and asked for art supplies. His artist's
eye told him Wren would be an excellent model, it
would help pass the time until he came up with a
better escape plan, and, it would distract Wren from
teaching him any of his acquired skills.

Wren's explanation of the daily schedule was spot
on. The Oompas came back to collect the breakfast
dishes and hand them white drawstring pants. It
dismayed Nels to find the pants quite diaphanous. The
bright sun did nothing to shield his anatomy from
anyone who cared to look, but at least the pants
offered a semblance of clothing. The fairy tale, "The
Emperor's New Clothes" popped into his mind as he
followed the artistically pleasing outline of Wren's ass
down the stairs to the garden.

Nels was following Wren into the open when one
of the large, silent men who'd been on the plane with
him stopped him with a hand to his bare chest. At
least, he thought he recognized the man. There'd been

times during the long flight when he'd surfaced from the drugs momentarily, and someone who looked like this man had given him another injection.

"Your master wants to see you," was all the man uttered as he barred the way outside.

"I don't care what *you* call him, but that sick fuck is not my master," came Nels's hot reply. He stopped his tirade when Wren came back inside and grabbed his hand.

"Please, Templar. Go with him. You don't want to anger this man. Meet with our master. He'll be nice to you, if you are nice to him. I will teach you what is required, I promise."

Glancing down at Wren's face, Nels found the boy genuinely afraid. He would've protested further, but Wren stepped closer and whispered into his ear, covering it with a kiss.

"Please don't do this, Templar. I don't want to lose you like the other boy before you. I'll explain when we're together again."

Reasoning it might indeed be better to be able to identify his mysterious buyer, Nels nodded and followed the man farther into the house. Before he turned the corner, he looked back to find Wren watching him with his arms wrapped around himself as if cold or very afraid.

Nels took in the sumptuously appointed room the man waved him into. There were two chaises for lounging, each topped with decorative pillows in jewel colors, and, between them, a low, round brass coffee table fluted like a pie crust, holding a silver coffee service. An ornate desk with a pristine top held a telephone and flat screen monitor. A black, executive chair completed the work station.

Through an inner door, he saw a king-sized bed made up with black satin sheets, he was just processing the alarming sight when another man walked through the door.

The man, dressed all in white with gold trim on his outer cloak, struck Nels as a Hollywood version of an Arab sheik. Short, dark hair, trimmed beard, black eyes, and hawkish nose completed the picture.

Nels widened his stance to hold his ground as whoever this man was walked around him like a man judging the attributes of a horse he wanted to buy. When they once again stood face-to-face, Nels couldn't hide a flinch when the man tugged on the drawstring of his pants to drop them to the ground.

Nels gritted his teeth. He wouldn't gift him with another display of unease. So far, the man hadn't laid a hand on him, but when he did, he'd be getting a nasty surprise because Nels deduced he now faced his purchaser.

The self-named Master turned to the man who'd ushered him into the room.

"Ah, Abdullah, I shall reward you well for suggesting this purchase. He's magnificent. Such pale hair and blue eyes. Aquamarines are the perfect stone to adorn him. And no tattoos to mar the perfection of his skin."

The man who'd escorted Nels bowed his head.

"Do you like the beard?" his purchaser went on. "As you know, I prefer much younger, beardless males, but I permitted this one because it gives him the appearance of one of those infidel Templars who defiled our holy al Aqsa mosque during the Crusades. I've named him Templar, and I hope Allah will be pleased when I break this one to my hand."

Nels saw a blazing firestorm of red. The man spoke about him as if he couldn't understand what was being said. Well, no one had ever equated him with a dumb animal, and he wouldn't let this man insult him. He found it hypocritical in the extreme for anyone to mention religion in a discussion of sexual perversion.

Not caring about the consequences, Nels spat out,

"You're a damned hypocrite if you're using Allah's name to condone what you are."

Nels rocked sideways. He hadn't seen the slap coming.

"You dare raise your voice to me, infidel," the master roared.

Nels clenched his fists and spat back, "I do dare. You dishonor your own religion. We both know what your intentions are. I'm not a practitioner of your religion, but I don't think it condones kidnapping a man for the purpose of buggery."

The Master whirled around and pointed to the other man in the room. 'Hold him, Abdullah."

Strong arms grabbed him from behind. He thought he'd be bent over and violated, but the master settled for fondling him, and none too gently.

"Oh I shall enjoy breaking you, Templar. My sweet little Wren is most talented, and pleases me well, but I'm in the mood for a challenge. Now, because of your insolence, you will be punished."

The master went to the door and returned with Mohammed who, before he changed places with Abdullah to hold him, handed him a supple wooden switch.

Nels struggled but soon found himself frog

marched to one of the chaises, stripped of his pants and sandals, and placed facedown on the chaise with his feet hanging over the edge. He began struggling in earnest when he heard the master say, "Five lashes on the bottom of each foot. The pain he feels when he walks should teach him respect when next he addresses me."

With the first whistling lash, Nels tried to pull away from a pain the likes of which he'd never known. He was gritting his teeth so hard, the only sound he made was a hiss that left his throat raw. He wanted to be brave. It was important to him. As Ross would say, bravery came embedded in his Viking DNA, but the next lash tore a sob from his mouth, and he realized Abdullah was hitting one foot at a time to prolong the punishment. He'd have to suffer through five lashes on each before the torture ended. The more he struggled, the harder Mohammed pressed him into the chaise. Perhaps he'd smother before the lashes ended. He would've chosen that over having his feet switched.

When Nels dared to raise his head, he watched through his tears as the master grinned and straightened his robe.

"You will find pleasing me a much less painful experience, Templar. Now, I'm going to go join Wren in the garden and tell him of your disobedience. I will also warn him the next time I call for you, you'd better greet me with a sweet mouth and willing body or he will be punished right along with you."

Turning to Abdullah, the master ordered. "When you've finished, have Mohammed take him back to his room. I want you to join me in the garden. I think my little bird might need some visual reinforcement to obey my orders."

Nels feared Wren might be in trouble as well, but he couldn't help him. Ah God, he wanted the beating to stop, and, he prayed it would end before he broke down and begged them. He'd lost count of the lashes but it felt like many, many more than ten had already been delivered.

***

Ross finished draping the camouflage net over his body, but froze when he spotted movement in the garden. He'd returned in the hour when the moon hung low on the horizon, and most people were in REM sleep, to dig a shallow pit in the palm grove and cover it with the net. Now he stretched out with his binoculars to his eyes. His parabolic mic picked up the

100

slight humming of a lithe young male walking around the edge of a swimming pool. Ross felt like a voyeur when the male removed his pants and sat on the side to braid his hair and dunk his feet in the water. His binoculars were of high enough magnification to pick up the piercings and bracelets, and the play of muscles in the male's back as he splashed water around.

He turned his binoculars on another male exiting the house. "Now here is the man I'm most interested in," he muttered. "Farrid, Prince al-Harbi's son-in-law. Handsome man, for a twisted kidnapper."

Ross held his breath as the man extended his hand and the swimmer left the pool to kneel before him. Ross checked the record button on his mic to be sure he wouldn't miss their conversation.

"Would you like me to please you this morning, Master?" Wren asked.

"I haven't decided, Wren. I'm not sure I should favor you this morning. I am most displeased. The Templar is, at this moment, being punished for his insolence. I gave you an order to teach him what I like and don't like, but you don't seem to have convinced him to cooperate. I won't tolerate insolence in any of my possessions. You have one week to train him."

Ross remained still as Farrid broke off the

harangue when another male joined them, the bigger of the two bodyguards who'd smuggled Nels out of the country.

He scrutinized the newcomer through his binoculars. From his size and muscular build, this man could handle himself in a fight, so his previous assumption Farrid had hired him as security seemed justified. In comparison, Farrid gave the impression of being soft and spoiled.

"Ah, Abdullah, I've just told Wren how displeased I am with him this morning, but I don't think he's aware of the consequences of my displeasure. If the Templar doesn't come to me without having to use coercion the next time I call for him, please show Wren what he will have to endure."

What Ross saw next almost made him leave his concealment and run, with gun drawn, to kill the bastard where he stood. Abdullah lifted his white *thawb* and, hitching the long dress-like garment to his waist, loosened the drawstring of his undergarment and let it drop to the ground. Abdullah's penis resembled a baseball bat in length and thickness.

Ross discarded the binoculars and picked up his camera, but almost didn't need its telephoto lens to see the stark fear painting the delicate boy's face. Actual photos would give him the proof he needed to convince Jack to give him some able-bodied assistants to spring Nels from this house.

Wren implored Farrid. "Please, Master, no. I'll try harder. I won't displease you, I promise. I'll make sure the Templar knows all of your desires. Just don't give me to Abdullah."

Wren clasped Farrid around his knees, and the man waved off his bodyguard, who picked up his underwear and tied it in place before letting his thawb drop back down as he returned to the house.

Ross's lens also captured Farrid's pleased expression when Wren turned to face him with tears running down his white cheeks. The boy cried without a sound, for the mic didn't record anything until Farid spoke again.

"Your pretty apology has put me in the mood to savor your talents, Wren. Unbind your glorious hair, my delight, and prepare me."

It took the boy several gulping breaths before he could answer. "Yes, Master,. I will pleasure you well this morning."

Wren removed the binding from the end of his long braid, and finger-combed his hair until it cascaded in liquid red-gold rivulets to his knees. He removed Farrid's outer garments with deliberation and sensual caresses, until the man stood nude before him. Dropping to his knees once again, Wren used his mouth and hands to harden the man's desire before leading him to one of the chaise lounges in the shade of the palm trees.

Ross stopped snapping pictures. He'd already seen more than enough, and the roiling of his stomach told him so. Since Farrid had a penchant for cutesy names, Ross hoped the Templar they referred to was Nels.

If he'd been able to snap a picture of Nels in the garden, he could've high-tailed it back to Riyadh to slap the proof on Jack's desk and demand an immediate extraction. The mention of punishment for the Templar's insolence made him uneasy. The fact Farrid granted the boy called Wren one more week to train the Templar at least assured him the man, despite punishment, still lived.

Several hours later, after a lunch of bottled water and a power bar, Ross grew drowsy with the heat until he spotted more movement in the garden. He'd already recorded an earlier conversation between Farrid and Abdullah, and knew Farrid expected an important visitor. He even knew refreshments of mint tea and honey cakes would be offered to the guest in the garden, but no names had been mentioned, and Abdullah and Mohammed, the other security guard he'd seen at BWI, had been cautioned to make themselves scarce after they saw to the refreshments.

Ross could tell Farrid, carrying an attaché case, sought to impress his guest from the deference he showed him as he led the way to chairs set up underneath a shady arrangement of palms. Ross picked up the camera and zoomed in on the stranger's face as soon as the man seated himself and moved the corner of his ghutra away from his face. He had to bite the inside of his lip to keep silent.

"I don't fucking believe it." Seated in Farrid's garden was none other than the man his team had tried to kill in Afghanistan last year. Rashid Ali al-Tikriti's face assaulted his eyes in living color. Al-Tikriti enjoyed the dubious honor of being the premier bomb manufacturer for any terrorist organization he chose to honor with his skill.

Rashid was a one-trick pony, so if Farrid was hosting him, he wanted something to go boom. Interesting, very interesting.

Ross snapped photos and adjusted the sound level on the mic. He wasn't missing a word of this conversation. He'd love to be able to tell his former team, even though they'd missed killing al-Tikriti with the Predator strike, it had at least destroyed what few handsome attributes the man possessed prior to having the mud hut he had been sleeping in vaporized. As they said in special operations, it hadn't been his day to die.

Now the left side of the bomb maker's face had a melted wax look from being severely burned, and the resulting scar tissue pulled his lower lip down to expose browned and missing teeth. Rashid looked like a gruesome jack-o'-lantern, helped along by missing part of his nose as well.

Suddenly nervous the bomb maker might be traveling with his own security, Ross lay perfectly still and scanned the area. Satisfied he remained undiscovered, he breathed easier but remained vigilant, triple checking the conversation was indeed recording.

Rashid accepted a glass of tea and selected a honey cake from the plate offered by Farrid. In the way of all Middle Eastern visits, he had to wait while the bomb maker complimented Farrid on being favored with four sons, and beautiful gardens, and the sweetness of the cakes. *C'mon, c'mon, get to the good stuff*. He focused when Rashid asked a direct question.

"I am here because you have requested my services. Would you care to tell me what you need done?"

"Yes," Farrid replied. "I am acting on behalf of Prince al-Harbi's middle son, Sabir. He is most upset his father, the king's liaison on the OPEC Council, is becoming too willing to let the infidel Americans have their way. He feels it's time his father stepped down from his position, in a manner of speaking."

"And I am to be the agent to retire the prince?"

"Yes, most definitely. The prince's seventieth birthday is in two weeks, and there will be a large party in his home. Unfortunately, Sabir will be traveling at that time, so he'll not be able to attend."

Rashid carefully set his empty glass down on the small table in front of him. "And what incentive do I have for helping Prince al-Harbi retire?"

Farrid reached down and picked up the metal attaché case he'd placed by his chair. "I have two hundred and fifty thousand US dollars in this case. It should be sufficient to buy whatever party favors you deem necessary. You'll receive an equal sum, wired to whatever financial institution you choose, once it's confirmed the prince has indeed retired."

"I'll need a diagram of the rooms and their dimensions in the prince's house to ensure the favors are placed accurately. What of you? Will you be in attendance?"

Farrid leaned toward the bomb maker. "Yes, I will. Of course, I'll need to know the precise time you intend to begin the celebration, so I can answer a convenient call of nature. You will need to be precise in your calculations. Sabir wants the main party room destroyed, not the rest of the house. Can you do so?"

Ross's camera recorded the blatant disdain on Rashid's face. "If I couldn't do it, you wouldn't be paying me this much money. Tell me, will there be women and children present?"

The question appeared to anger Farrid, who straightened his posture. "Don't concern yourself. Our wives will be there, but not our children. It's to be an adult party."

Rashid continued to probe. "And you are prepared to make such a sacrifice?"

"The sacrifice is worth the gain. Sabir is confident the king will award him his father's position, to ease his sorrow, and I will be given a commensurate reward by Sabir, as we work to sabotage what plans the Americans have to steal our oil and our wealth. We are both men in our prime and quite capable of attracting new, younger wives.

"I can have the diagram of the prince's house for you in one week. Return here at the same time as today, and we'll discuss how your entry into the prince's house can be effected."

"Holy shit, holy shit, *holy shiit,*" Ross had to get the pictures and recordings back to Jack Adams, asap, but not before he moved closer to the tower room this night. He needed to verify Nels was there before he took his information back to Riyadh. It would give him the leverage he needed to accompany the strike team when they took down Rashid and Farrid in one week's time.

# Chapter Eight

The bastard Mohammed made him walk
unassisted back to the tower room. It was a measure of
pride he hadn't fallen upon the bed until the man left
the room, but now Nels curled into a fetal position and
let his tears flow. In all his life, he'd never been
subjected to such punishment, and it been a blow to
his psyche. In desperation, Nels called out to the one
friend he thought could help him. *Please, Ross, find
me. You said you're very good at finding things, so
find me. Oh God, find me and take me away from
here.*

Just thinking of how shockingly fast his life had
gone from normal to horror show awful broke his
Danish reserve, and left him unable to stifle the
racking sobs. Cold compresses placed on his feet
finally calmed him. He hadn't heard Wren enter the
room.

"Shhh, Templar, I'll make it better for you. It'll be
painful to walk for a few days, but I can take some of
the sting away with this cintment. Come now, stop
crying, please stop crying."

Nels fell docile as Wren applied an analgesic ointment to the soles of his feet. He even let him wash the tear-streaked kohl from his face, and didn't protest when Wren crawled up on the bed to cradle his head in his lap.

He must've fallen asleep, thanks to Wren's talented fingers running through his hair, because the next sensation he felt was a gentle shake.

"Wake up, Templar. The Oompas have brought dinner. You need to eat. I know this has been a hard day, but you need to eat. You don't even have to sit up. I'll feed you."

Nels opened his mouth to say he wanted no part of dinner, but he couldn't speak around the bite of roasted lamb Wren swiftly popped into his mouth. His bruised nerve endings might not care to eat, but his stomach was totally onboard with the idea. Sitting up, Nels reached for another piece of meat and received a beatific smile from Wren as he did so.

Nels ate the rest of the meal in silence, but felt increasingly guilty for not at least thanking Wren for his care. He could tell by his furtive glances the boy was seriously worried about something, and he flashed back to Wren's plea for cooperation right before his meeting with the master.

"Tell me what trouble I've gotten us into," Nels croaked. He had to take a sip of pomegranate juice to clear the frog in his throat.

His question apparently killed Wren's appetite, for the boy dabbed his mouth with the linen napkin and rose to pace the tower room. The artist in Ross just couldn't help appreciating the play of muscles on the nude form as the boy moved with the litheness of a pacing panther. He'd pluck out his tongue before he told Wren so, but it was a real pleasure to watch him move.

"I told you, Templar, I was assigned to teach you how to please our master. When you made him angry today, he used Abdullah to show me what would happen to me if you don't comply. I've been given one more week to sweeten your attitude, or I'll be severely punished."

"What? Did that big goon Abdullah wave the wooden cane he used on me at you, or did he have an actual weapon? I don't think the master...." Nels had to loosen his jaw, which had clamped down tight at the sobriquet used by their captor, before he could continue. "I don't think the master would hurt you, Wren. You're too beautiful and talented for him to break."

He reared back in surprise when Wren threw himself into his arms.

"You are very, very wrong, Templar. I am broken, I've been broken twice. Once before I ever came here, and I don't ever care to be broken again. Abdullah did flash a weapon at me. He dropped his trousers and showed me his genitals."

"And that frightened you?" After everything the boy had been through, it seemed unlikely.

"No, don't scoff at what you don't understand. The man is abnormally large. He could service horses, and they'd be completely satisfied when he finished. The master told me he'd let Abdullah take me if you resisted his next advance. And, believe me, Abdullah wouldn't be gentle with me. He'd hurt me, Templar. He likes hurting people. I can tell."

The boy trembled at the thought of being given to Abdullah. "Shhh, Wren. I won't let Abdullah hurt you."

Nels rocked the boy until the trembling stopped, and then cast around for some way of making the big, ugly, scary monster in the room disappear. His eyes landed on the bookcase overflowing with Wren's collection of printed treasures.

"What are you reading now? Would you like me to read to you?" He sighed in relief when Wren sat up with an interested expression on his face.

"Would you? I'm working my way through all of Shakespeare's plays. I finished Othello and thought I'd read Macbeth next."

"Ah the Bard, I know him well. Shall we play the parts? I'll say a line, and you say a line, but you can play the feminine roles. Your handsome face and lovely tresses would've wooed the crowds at the Globe Theater."

"Do you think I'm attractive, Templar?"

*Aaargh, stepped on your tongue, you did, Nels Kirkegaard.* "Fishing for compliments, Wren? You don't need me to verify what your mirror tells you every morning." He stifled a groan of pain as he hobbled from the bed to the chaise. "Come now, 'Act I. Scene I. An open place. Thunder and lightning. Enter the three witches.' I'll play the first witch. 'When shall we three meet again, in thunder, lightning, or in rain?'"

"You're not even looking at the book, Templar. How do you know the lines?"

"I've already read the play, and if I read it once, I can recall it forever more. So, you take the book, and I'll speak my lines after yours."

As a diversion, Shakespeare won hands down. Wren and he exchanged lines for the rest of the day, and, after a break for dinner, long into the night, until the play ended. Giving in to Wren's exuberance, they even acted out the scenes, with him giving Wren stage directions. He had to hand it to the boy. If they ever won their freedom, Wren could play a convincing Lady Macbeth.

Thoroughly exhausted, the budding actor named Wren bade him good night and cuddled up to sleep.

Nels envied his ability to put worry behind him. While the boy slept, Nels's, brain ran like a hamster in an exercise wheel. He knew, deep down, Wren hadn't lied, and the master would hurt Wren if he continued to offer resistance. He'd seen the sadistic grin on the man's face when he ordered Abdullah to cane him.

He also recalled Wren's mention of a previous inhabitant of the tower room who did nothing but cry and, one day, never came back. He wasn't naïve enough to think the boy had been given his freedom.

And so, he cast his eyes to the screen-covered window, and offered a final prayer for the evening. *Please, Ross, find us. Find us soon.*

He'd let Wren teach him, but at what cost to himself?

\*\*\*

Under cover of night, Ross crept close to the smooth wall of the tower, and now lay in a stone-strewn *wadi* with his parabolic mic pointed at the screened window. From his position, he could make out the pattern of flowers and birds in the screen from the light shining through it.

He'd been eager to hear the sound of his friend's voice, but what he heard didn't make a whole lot of sense. Ross removed the earbuds and blew on them to make sure they'd picked up the conversation accurately. The voices sounded like English speakers, but in an archaic way. Ross filtered out the odd syntax and knew Nels had spoken those lines.

"If it were done—when 'tis done—then 'twere well...." He recognized Nels's voice with his distinctive Oxford accent, but where had he heard those words before?

He continued to listen until he heard the line offered in what must be the boy's voice. "We fail? But screw your courage to the sticking place. And we'll not fail."

Ah ha, they were reciting Shakespeare's Macbeth. Ross made himself a promise to buy tickets for all of them to the next performance in Washington's

116

Kennedy Center if he got Nels out of this alive.

He packed up his gear in preparation for his return to Riyadh, wishing he could send some sort of signal to his friend, but he couldn't risk it. He couldn't afford to alert Farrid to the fact his little hideaway had been discovered.

He did spare a final glance up at the window to offer silent encouragement. *Hang in there, buddy. The cavalry is on the way. One more week. Do whatever you need to do. Just hang in there for one more week.*

Ross couldn't call lying in bed and staring at the ceiling of his hotel room sleeping, so he had to will himself, despite his frayed temper, to keep his face pleasant and not fidget the next morning while he waited for Jack Adams's secretary to tell him he could see the man. With his last reserve of patience, he smiled at the woman as she held the door open for him, but, once the door closed behind him, all restraint disappeared, and he interrupted Jack's pleasant greeting.

"We need to discuss this in a SCIF, or whichever other secure room you have. The rescue of my friend has just gotten more complicated."

"Goddamn it, Lassie. You and your special friends

117

are like a rash. Every time I think I've gotten rid of it, it comes back and it costs my Uncle Sam a lot of money to make it go away again. Shit! Follow me."

Ross followed Jack to a room containing the necessary security. The password and identity check needed to even open the door told him they could speak freely once inside. When Jack took a chair and stared at him with a "well here we are, spill" expression, Ross cued his tape recorder to the conversation between Farrid and the bomb maker.

"The guy Farrid is paying to help retire Prince al-Harbi during his upcoming birthday party is Rashid Ali al-Tikriti. I think he's among the top five people our mutual uncle wants to make take a prolonged dirt nap thanks to his expertise with explosives. My team and I thought we'd gotten him last year in a Predator strike, but we were never able to confirm it. I have the pictorial proof here we missed him."

Jack cursed. "Go on."

"You'll need to get one of your tech gurus in here to download my photos. I know how to do it, but I don't want to chance messing it up. I've also got photographic evidence Farrid is twisted, which should make his father-in-law doubly happy when you inform him his middle son, Sabir, also wants to off him."

Jack reached into his pocket and put a chewable antacid in his mouth before asking, "What of your friend? Is he the one you photographed with Farrid?"

"No, I don't know who he is, other than Farrid called him Wren. He appears to be in his late teens, early twenties, to me. I don't think the sex I took pictures of was strictly consensual, because right before he went down on Farrid, the perv threatened him with bodily harm if he didn't perform up to snuff."

"Do you even have proof your friend is there?"

"While I don't have photographic evidence, I did record his voice talking to Wren later that evening. I also discovered Nels has already been punished once for resisting becoming Farrid's new squeeze toy."

Ross played the tape in its entirety before saying, "As you heard, the bomb maker will return in one week for the layout of the prince's house. If we do this right, we can take him and get Nels back at the same time. I know my former team would love the chance to put a big, black X through Rashid's wanted poster."

Jack Adams didn't give him any further feedback on the recordings. He simply picked up the phone and barked for someone named Stan to get his ass into the secure room, ASAP. He didn't even blink at Ross until he'd reviewed the photographs several times as Ross identified the subjects for him. His sole comment came on an indrawn breath when Abdullah dropped his trousers.

"Abdullah is one sick puppy. I can see why you want to get your friend away as soon as possible. Now go back to your hotel, Lassie, and wait for me to contact you. I need to take this upstairs so the ambassador can hash it out with the elephants in Washington."

"Okay, Jack, I'll go without a fuss, if you assure me I can go in with whoever is sent to take out Farrid and the bomb-maker. You owe me for alerting you first, rather than going in like a one-man wrecking crew. I don't even care if you can't give me a weapon, but I need to be there for Nels. This has to have been a traumatic experience for him, and I want him to see a familiar, compassionate face when the balloon goes up."

"And if I can't?"

"Well then, in the next day or so Nels will get rescued by me alone, the prince will have a dead son-in-law, and the bomb-maker will be free to attend the prince's birthday."

"You won't be able to do anything if I have you arrested, Lassie?"

"Don't play pissing games with me, Jack. You know I'm capable of making good my threat. I know you're capable of invoking some Homeland Security regulation to keep me confined for some time, but why go through all of the hassle?

"Jack, I'm well aware I'm no longer on a team, but with my training I'm not John Q. Public, either. I need to be there for my friend. I haven't been out of the service for so long I've forgotten my training. And I do know how to stay out of the way and obey any orders the team leader gives me. Let me be there for him, please, Jack."

Jack made him grin when he scratched the back of his neck before cursing. "I knew that fucking rash would come back, but at least, being stationed in an Arabic country, there's no chance it's a symptom of an STD. Get the hell out of here and wait for my call. And, no, you don't need to remind me of the timetable for the bomb maker's next visit to Farrid."

Letting Jack keep the photos and recordings, Ross left the embassy to begin the hurry- up and wait part of an impending mission. He considered drinking his breakfast to pass the time, but in no way did he want to impair his ability to respond to the call whenever it came. He decided to grab a light breakfast, catch a few

The Danegeld

Zs, and hit the well-equipped gym in his hotel, instead.

# Chapter Nine

Hands skimmed up the insides of his thighs, and Nels parted his legs in silent invitation. He'd been wanting this to happen for months. He moaned when a warm, wet tongue laved his dick, and arched to offer himself. *Oh yes, please. Ahh, don't stop. God, that feels exquisite, but go slower, it's been so long I don't think I can....*

Nels opened his eyes and saw he was spread-eagled and dead center on the tree of life rug in Ross's great room. Much to his horror, he had an audience. The pretty Jamaican barista grinned down at him and offered a to-go cup.

"Good morning, Mister Nels. You'll be needing this triple espresso."

As he twisted his head away in mortification, a flash of light from above startled him, and he lifted his hand to shield his eyes. A large cameras suspended from the ceiling recorded his every move, and he tried but failed to bat away his lover's hands when he heard someone order a closeup of his genitals.

His lover didn't seem upset to perform in public,

because the warm mouth and silky hand had not ceased drawing him closer to release. Nels marshaled all his willpower to reach down to stay his unidentified lover's hands and demand he stop. Making love in front of an audience went against his Danish proprieties. When his hands tugged at long, silky hair, Nels's eyes flew open for real.

Thank Odin, he'd been dreaming. He wasn't in Ross's house at all. The barista standing on the sidelines, and the director demanding they replay the scene, had been figments of his imagination, But Wren's mouth and hands working him were real. He shook the boy's shoulders and shouted Wren's name to get his attention, but it didn't distract the talented houri, who inserted the tip of his finger between his cheeks, and Nels erupted like one of those star cluster fireworks. A loud hiss in his ascendance, and multiple, spectacular starbursts, until he lay spent and trembling.

"Wow, I've never heard my name shouted in passion before," Wren chuckled.

Nels tried to turn on his side but couldn't manage it. He lay sprawled and gasping but did manage breath enough to say, "It wasn't passion. I was asleep, and you startled me awake."

Wren pouted. "Well, we're equal, then, because you startled me awake when you snugged your erect dick into my ass early this morning. I woke up to you kissing my back and fondling me. I thought you'd decided to let me teach you, so I reciprocated."

Nels's cheeks heated.

"Come on, Templar. Don't be ashamed. I know you enjoyed it. You must not have regular sex, because you came far too quickly."

He ran his finger down the slickness of Nels's chest and tsked. "Come, let me help you into the shower. The Oompas will be bringing breakfast soon, and, as much as I like to admire my handiwork, I don't like a sweaty dining companion."

Wanting to put some distance between himself and Wren, he stood and collapsed in pain. He'd forgotten about the caning. He'd need help to get to the shower, and to the garden for exercise. Wren was just the right height to support him down the steps and to the side of the pool.

Swimming laps usually relaxed him. He could zone out, enjoy the feel of the water sliding over his body, and concentrate on breathing on the fourth stroke, but not today. What had happened this morning depressed him. Wren thought he'd given in, and he had, but Nels couldn't get over the guilt. Though Wren was a boy in a man's body, albeit a boy with an adult's sexual experience, he was still a boy who'd been forced into a life not of his choosing. He had eleven years on Wren, and had had the opportunity to choose his own sexual partners. Christ, he didn't even know if Wren had ever made love to a woman. Well, since he'd come to the master at the age of eleven, odds were he hadn't.

Nels stopped swimming when it dawned on him belaboring the point now was moot because free choice wasn't an option for either one of them.

He waded to the side of the pool and cradled his head in his hands to call himself the name he'd wanted to say all morning. Hypocrite. He'd let Wren teach him to keep the master from punishing him, but, deep down, he knew the reason behind his acquiescence.

***

Nels lagged behind returning to their room, and Wren raced toward what the Oompas left on the bed.

"Our master has given you what you asked for." He handed over the sketchpad and box of charcoal pencils.

"And there is even another box containing watercolors and brushes. Holding up a gummy, gray square, Wren asked, "What's this for?"

"It's an artist's eraser."

Nels eased himself into a sitting position on the bed. On the walk back from the pool, they'd discovered he could manage without Wren's assistance if he walked at the speed of a snail.

"Would you like me to sketch you?"

Wren grinned. "Would you? Where shall I sit? What pose do you want me in? "Of course this will be a nude portrait."

Nels stopped laughing long enough to order, "I want you over by the window, sitting cross-legged and brushing your beautiful hair."

After Wren had complied with alacrity, Nels directed the placement of his arms, legs, and hair, and gave him a final order before he put the charcoal pencil into action.

"Now hold your pose and don't fidget. I'll sketch you as fast as I can but it will take some time."

Wren proved to be an excellent model. He held the pose for a long while, his hair now gleaming in the sunlight from the thorough brushing he'd given it.

Finally at the end of his patience, he asked.

"C'mon, Templar, can't we take a break? My ass and legs are numb, and I want to see what you've drawn."

In response, Nels held out the small metal cup, that'd come with the watercolors.

"You can stop posing and fill this cup with water. I'm finished sketching, but you can't view it until I've added a few more details. I'll show you when I'm finished."

Wren did as he was asked then wandered over to his bookcase and picked up a book on physics. He sat on the floor by the bottom of the bed studying the book until Nels tugged his hair.

"You can see it now, if you want."

An exclamation burst from him as soon as he saw the portrait. "Oh my God, it's me, and I'm gorgeous." Wren's finger hovered over the red of his hair and the small dabs of emerald green color representing the stones in his rings and bracelets, but he questioned the expression on his face. "Do I really smile like that?"

"Yes, you do, especially right before you get up to some mischief, or say something outrageous. Uh, oh, there it is again. What are you about, Wren?"

"Well, I'm thinking we could both use some exercise. Drawing and posing can put a kink in the muscles, and you owe me for this morning."

"I thought my sketch payment enough for this morning."

"As a thank you, yes, it is, but as exercise? Nope, you left me unsatisfied. The master wants me to teach you, but reciprocity is also included in the plan. I teach you what pleases our master, and you please me in return."

Crawling on all fours toward the artist in a panther-worthy stalk, Wren waited until he closed the sketchpad and removed the art supplies to the floor next to the bed before he pounced. Fluttering his long lashes, he whispered, "Why don't we start with a kiss?"

Despite the immediate case of nerves the question engendered, Nels roared with laughter when Wren elaborated, "I mean on the lips this time."

"As my master commands."

The hypnotic effect of the younger man's clear, green eyes overwhelmed him with the need to give Wren as much honesty as he could. He may be a self-proclaimed hypocrite, but he wanted to be an honest one as well. Gathering Wren into his arms, he leaned down and nuzzled the side of his neck.

Using the Titian-red tresses to shield his lips from the cameras, he whispered, "I will do as you bid me, Wren. I will follow your every direction on how the master likes to be serviced, but let's call it what it is. It's sex, not love. The Templar may please the master when he summons him, but right here, right now Nels Kirkegaard will be making love to Wren. When I touch you, I want my name to be in your mind. Nels. My name is Nels." And he began by showing the delicate bird how a man could call him to hand just by puckering his lips.

Wren proved to be demonstrative as well as vocal, and Nels soon found himself so hard and aching it blinded him to all but the feel of warm hands and lips on his body. But, when he flipped Wren over on his stomach, reality doused him with a bucketful of cold water.

What the hell? He'd been about to pull Wren's ass into position and ram his dick in to the hilt when his conscience knocked some sense into him. Instead, he smoothed a trembling hand down Wren's back and rolled away from him. When Wren flipped right over and stretched himself head-to-toe over his body to bite his earlobe hard, it shocked him.

"Oh fuck no, Nels. I'm not letting you have a case of nerves now. I'm so hard I could pound nails with my dick. I forbid you to give me another case of blue balls. I've suffered all damned day wanting to feel you inside me. I want this. I need this. Please, Nels, please, please, please. If you need to think of me as someone else, I don't fucking care. Scream any name you want until the Oompa Loompas come to make sure we aren't killing each other, but don't stop now."

His sincerity persuaded him. Guilt would have to wait until he could think with his bigger brain.

Nels grabbed him around the waist and rolled him once again to his stomach. Wren complied with alacrity when he gave him a small nudge, and his lovely, firm ass rose before him, and he seated himself with a fluid thrust of his hips.

Like the baseball game he'd watched with Ross, he filled all the bases, and then hit a long drive over the fence. Wren's scream of "*Templar*" brought him sliding into home base, and the name he'd wanted to call for some time now escaped from his throat. He had enough brain cells left to remember his post-coital manners and pulled Wren into his arms before succumbing to sleep.

\*\*\*

Farrid set his coffee cup back into the saucer and leaned closer to the television monitor. His attention stood fast on the two men as they wound themselves around each other in the age-old game of sex. *Hmm, Templar is good, very good. Maybe I've been wrong to keep my appetite confined to young boys. It might be amusing to have Wren join us when I know I can trust Templar not to do anything foolish.*

His own dick demanded attention when the Templar mounted Wren from behind, and his hand kept the rhythm of his captive's thrusts. Unknown to his slaves, it became a trifecta finish. His release put him into a mellow mood, until he remembered he'd be spending the next two days at his other home, listening to his wife complain about his frequent absences. The thought of the surprise he and Sabir had planned put him back into his happy zone, and he switched off the monitor and headed for his bathroom.

# Chapter Ten

Ross's pace burned rubber on the hotel treadmill until someone hopped onto the one next to him. He didn't bother glancing over at the person who'd almost broken his concentration, because he didn't want to spare a second in planning how to get Nels out of Farrid's compound. A tap on his shoulder almost made him growl, and he had to grab the safety bars to keep from falling off the back end of the damned machine when he realized who'd broken his concentration. He fumbled to turn off the treadmill.

"I see you're still grace personified, Dawg."

Ross swiped the sweat out of his eyes and gaped at the Troll. "Please tell me this is a professional visit and not a serendipitous meeting."

"Serendipitous?" Troll scoffed. "My, my, you must've had time to read a dictionary since you retired. No, this is serious, not serendipitous."

Glancing around to make sure they had the gym all to themselves, Troll continued. "The guys and I endured eight hours on a plane from Kabul to get here, and we didn't come for R&R. Why don't we go back to your room so you can clean up, and we'll grab some lunch before going to see our uncle. Geez, Lassie, I thought you'd behave once you got out, but you seem to have shot my theory all to hell."

Ross knew the drill, there'd be no talking about anything connected to the bomb maker until they returned to the embassy's secure conference room, so he willed himself to give the appearance of a casual diner. But if someone ever interrogated him on what he'd ordered or eaten for lunch he'd be unable to recall a single thing.

Troll, on the other hand, ordered with an eye to Uncle Sam's expense account, and Ross couldn't blame him. If things went to hell during the mission, it might well be his last meal.

As he waited for Troll to scarf down his lunch, Ross couldn't help falling back into the old team mannerisms. "Your beard makes a statement, Troll. Put a checkered headdress on, and a flowing robe, and you could pass for a native. What did you do, spend your time sunbathing and avoiding barbers on your last assignment?"

Troll gave as good as he got. "Fuck you very much, Lassie. Have you gotten close to a mirror lately? Nice beard, by the way. It gives you a dashing, thief-of-the-desert image. I hear the Sheik of Araby trend will hit Omaha next year."

Ross batted his eyelashes at the man before getting serious. "Thanks for coming. I'm glad it'll be you guys up at bat."

Troll laughed. "Jack didn't greet us with open arms. He says the sole reason he let you persuade him to ask for us is because we get things done fast. He also says we give his balls a rash whenever we're in close proximity to his office."

"Don't know about you, Troll, but I'd rather have a rash on my balls than my balls in a nutcracker, if I was stupid enough to use the wrong tool for the job."

Troll wiped his mouth on his napkin and placed it beside his empty plate. "Too true, Dawg, too true. Let's settle the bill and get the hell out of here. The rest of the team and our guest lecturer should have made it to the embassy by now."

Ross did a double take when he found the guest lecturer to be none other than Prince al-Harbi. The patriarch had old school Bedouin evident in his erect posture, extreme reserve, and very large, very prominent hooked nose. He shook the man's hand when Jack introduced him.

Jack started the ball rolling. "Okay, now that we

have everyone gathered, I want Ross to tell us why he came here, and what he found once he arrived. Save your questions until he's finished. I've already briefed Prince al-Harbi, but he wanted to hear the details in person."

He handed Ross a remote control and informed him the photos were loaded up on the computer with the sound meshed up with them then pointed to Stan, who was sitting in the corner of the room in case his technical expertise was needed, to reassure Ross nothing would be lost.

Falling back into his military briefer mode, Ross didn't use a lot of adjectives just the bare, bitter facts. He did notice the prince stiffen when the picture of Farrid and Wren flashed on the screen and, since he knew a few Arabic curse words, Ross recognized his muttered epithet as being singularly descriptive and vile.

He ended the brief with exterior shots of the compound, and the reminder Rashid al-Tikriti would visit Farrid in three days. "If we want to take this guy out, we'll need to do it after he leaves Farrid's compound. As much as I'd like to do this the easy way, and level the whole place with a well-placed drone strike, I don't want to risk killing my friend or the other man being held captive." He looked around at the rapt faces. "That completes my brief. Questions?"

Otter spoke up. "For his initial visit, did Rashid have anyone else with him? Did he have a driver or other security personnel?"

"No. He drove himself to the meeting." Ross fast forwarded through the pictures he'd collected, until a shot of a black Range Rover with tinted windows showed up. "That's the car he used for the meeting."

Otter rubbed his hands together. "Nice. It has lots of room to reach underneath and attach things."

Everyone in the room, except maybe the prince, knew what type of accessories Otter liked to attach to cars. Rashid al-Tikriti used the same ones.

"Okay, that takes care of the bomb maker, but how do we get inside the compound without risking the lives of the captives?" Ross asked, the question foremost on his mind.

"I know how." Prince al-Harbi's deep voice had all eyes swinging to him. "I'm assuming you're not going to take out the bomb maker until he's away from the compound. If we time it correctly, once he clears the long drive to Farrid's house, you can kill him any way you like. I will send my man along with however many others you deem necessary to call upon Farrid. They will act as security for my man, who will be carrying a sizeable sum of money."

He smiled, but the grim line did not depict humor. "Farrid will be expecting the delivery. I'll arrange a call to him the day before to tell him it's an OPEC Fund for International Development installment for one of the African members who accepts such payments as the benefit of doing business with us. He will be led to think the call is coming from Sabir's staff, and since the money must be delivered to him in such a narrow window of time, he'll have to accept it at his compound or miss his scheduled meeting with the bomb maker. Once inside, you can determine the right time to kill Farrid and his two bodyguards for yourselves.

Prince al-Harbi looked away and then back to catch Ross's eye. "I would do the deed myself, but that insect is married to my daughter, and even though his sexual perversion has dishonored her, I don't want his blood on my hands when I hold my grandsons. My man will stay behind and sanitize the house. I want no evidence left behind to embarrass my daughter or our family name."

Jack Adams spoke next. "What about your son, Sabir?"

The prince adjusted he robes. "Ah, yes, Sabir. He's

already left for a meeting in Vienna, the one guaranteeing he'll miss my birthday celebration. You needn't concern yourself with Sabir. He won't be returning from that trip. His penchant for fast cars will finally be the death of him."

Ross looked at Troll and the rest of the team and knew they were all thinking the same thing. You couldn't beat Bedouin justice for putting a period at the end of a death sentence.

The prince stood to bring the meeting to a close. "Mr. Adams has my number. Just tell me when you need my man to report to you, and it shall be done. You needn't worry about him being squeamish or incapable of following your orders. He's one of my best security men. The SAS trained him, and he learned his lessons well."

After Jack Adams left to escort the prince out, Gunner cracked them all up. "If I had the prince for a father-in-law, I'd be the most faithful bastard in the world."

Ross waited until the laughter stopped to ask the important question he'd held on the tip of his tongue all day. "I am going along on this op, aren't I?"

"Yeah, Lassie you are. You spotted Rashid for us." Holding up his hand when Ross tried to speak, Troll continued. "And, despite Jack's strenuous objections, you'll be armed."

Ross let out a sigh of relief as his former teammate went on.

"Now, let me sketch out the plan for taking down Farrid, and anyone who has any better ideas, feel free to jump in. Part of the plan will involve Lassie and Gunner taking a ride out to Farrid's compound. Gunner, you'll be guarding Otter with your long gun while he plays mechanic, so you'll need to get the lay of the land to determine distances and best shooting angles. After Rashid's car leaves, you get to play bodyguard for the prince's man with Lassie and Otter.

Troll turned to his EOD expert. "Otter, you do what you do best. I'm figuring you can play with Rashid's car while he's meeting with Farrid. Make sure it doesn't go boom until he's well off the road to the compound. We wouldn't want to alarm Farrid by deconstructing his recent guest within hearing range, so I'll be the one with the remote control waiting for his car to pass by.

*\*\**

Being kissed awake didn't happen very often to

Nels, and neither did the rasp of a man's beard on his cheek. Opening his eyes, he had to back away a little to bring Wren into focus. He studied the faint reddish stubble on the man's cheek before asking, "I've never seen a beard on you before, Wren. What do you do, sneak out of bed and pluck it out before I wake up?"

His question seemed to startle Wren who reached up and ran his hand over his face.

"Ah, the Oompa Loompas will soon be spiking my pomegranate juice for a waxing session. The master does not appreciate beard burn." He looked thoughtful. "Hmm, if I've got hair on my face, I wonder where else it's sprouted?"

Nels chuckled in semi-embarrassed amusement when Wren grabbed his hand and cupped it around his balls. However, when he made to move away, Wren deepened his voice and demanded, in a fair imitation of the master's voice, "Prepare me, Templar."

When his eyes flew to Wren's face, the man gave him a stone-cold demand. "Your mouth will harden me, and I will take you this morning, Templar. You will perform to my satisfaction, or you'll once again suffer punishment."

He knew the reason behind the command, but he didn't have to like it. It made him flash back to the dream of performing on command in front of an audience on Ross's rug, and his morning erection deflated as suddenly as a balloon bumping into a needle.

His blush turned his entire body red. "Sorry, Wren, but I can't perform on command for someone I have no affection for. As much as I don't want to see either one of us punished, I can't command my dick to be happy about pleasing the master."

"I thought this might happen." Wren rolled over and picked up a small jar from the floor next to the bed. Taking a dab of cream from the jar, Wren ordered, "Hold still. The master told me this is made from ground up beetles when he had to use it on me to instruct me. It will enable you to perform, no matter how much your dick wants to disobey."

Nels attempted to bat his hands away, but Wren persisted. Before he could object, the cream slid up his dick from base to head.

Wren hadn't exaggerated. Within a matter of moments, he had a rock-hard erection burning for relief. "Fucking hell! Let me up, Wren. I need to wash this off."

"Apt choice of words, but washing won't help. Relief will come when you've used your dick long and hard. Obvious pun intended. Now, let's take it from the top. Prepare me Templar."

If relief would come through use, Nels cast his personal squeamishness aside and used his hands to pleasure Wren.

"No, harder. Squeeze my balls harder. The master likes a little pain with his pleasure. Ooh, right, he'll like what you just did. Nooo, don't bite him there. He doesn't care for being bitten there. But you can try that on me, anytime."

Nels got so caught up in the instructions, Wren had to bark at him, "Turn over, Templar, and grab the headboard."

His big brain screamed *no*, but his smaller one chanted, *yes, yes, yes. I want relief.* He flinched when Wren rubbed something liquid between his cheeks, and hoped to hell he'd applied lubricant, not more of the beetle guts. He flinched again when Wren's body covered his. "No, Wren, stop. I don't want to do this. We shouldn't be doing this. I'm sorry, but..."

Wren put his lips next to his ear and whispered, "I know, Nels. I know. Shhh. I wish I didn't have to insist, but our master will call for you soon, and you need to get over your reluctance. No, don't clench. I'll hurt you if you clench. You must concentrate, now, and call his name and no other's when you come."

After squeezing his eyes shut, Nels obeyed his teacher. His emotions had flatlined, and he didn't have the strength to knock Wren's hands away when he used a warm washcloth to clean him. The sound of a sniffle made his eyes spring open again. "Why are you crying, Wren?"

"Because you hate me, now. I wanted us to be friends, but I'm a coward. I wanted a friend, but I don't want to be hurt by Abdullah. I forced you so I wouldn't be hurt."

The tears eviscerated him. He couldn't blame the boy. Neither of them had control of his own life anymore. Opening his arms, Nels asked, "Would you let me hold you? I need someone to hold. I don't hate you. I need someone to hold onto right now, and who better than my friend?"

With a sob, Wren complied and threw himself into his arms. With no one to chastise his unmanly behavior, Nels combined the younger man's tears with his own. He cried not because he'd given in, but in sorrow over two lives lost before they'd had a chance to mature. Even though he didn't pray often, his despair found the words for him. *Please, God, let Ross find me.*

# Chapter Eleven

Farrid paced his office in agitation. He'd married a stupid, fat, whining cow. Four babies had left her stomach spongy and her thighs dimpled with fat, and she was too stupid to see his distaste each time he mounted her. Thank Allah the call concerning a payment to one of the greedy Africans had given him an excuse, under the pretense of work, to return to the peace of his special compound. He didn't like having to use his compound for the transaction, but there wouldn't be enough time to keep his meeting with the bomb maker and then meet the man, Suliman, who'd be delivering the OPEC money, unless he met both at his private compound. He had to make sure the bomb maker had the diagram of the prince's house and got well away before Sabir's man arrived with the money.

He calmed himself with the thought he soon wouldn't need to close his eyes and imagine the feel of young, firm, muscled flesh beneath him in order to perform his duties. He might not even take a new wife too soon. It would be to his benefit if people thought him in deep mourning over the loss of his father-in-

law and his wife. He'd have to make damn sure
Suliman didn't discover he had special residents in the
tower room.

Thinking of his sequestered treasures led him to
his monitor, and he sat back to verify how well Wren
heeded his command to teach the Templar. The sight
of their bodies wrapped around each other excited
him, until he saw Wren burst into tears, and the
Templar open his arms and rock the boy to sleep with
kisses.

Rage overwhelmed him. His little bird's affections
had been co-opted by the blond infidel. Such rebellion
needed an immediate, painful response. Opening his
office door, he called for Abdullah.

Not waiting for the man to inquire why he'd been
summoned, Farrid got right to it. "I want you to tell
Mohammed to bring the Templar to me. Mohammed
will stay to ensure my safety. I've decided to give you
the reward I promised you. Once Mohammed brings
the Templar to me, you may use Wren to your
satisfaction. Heed me well, Abdullah. I don't want him
disfigured or unable to perform after you finish with
him, but I want you to remind Wren I am the master. I
own him, and he stays alive by my sufferance."

Abdullah bowed. "Thank you. It will be my

pleasure to convey your message to Wren."

***

Fresh from his shower, Nels sat on the bed and enjoyed the picture Wren made as he braided his hair. Nels admired his meticulousness about keeping his red-gold glory shiny and flowing into waves when it dried and he let it loose in a shimmering feast for the eyes. Just as Wren secured the end with an elastic band, the door swung open, and Mohammed stepped in, carrying the usual thin, white trousers.

"The master has sent for the Templar," Mohammed said as he tossed the pants into Nels's lap. "Dress, and I'll escort you."

"But the Master said he'd give me a week to train the Templar, and there are two days left."

Mohammed spat his contempt. "You don't question the master, ever. If he commands it, it will be done."

Nels rose to his feet and drew Wren's eyes. "That's okay. I can handle this. Don't worry. You won't be punished because of me."

Wren rose from where he'd been sitting on the floor. "Templar, you will follow me to the bathroom, and I will prepare you." As he passed the bed, he grabbed the trousers and marched into the bathroom, calling over his shoulder, "Since this is his first time with the master, he's nervous. He needs to void his bladder so he doesn't disgrace himself."

Nels would've protested his bladder didn't need emptying, but the caution in Wren's eyes stopped him from speaking, and he followed the swaying braid in front of him. He skidded to a stop when he saw what Wren had in mind for him as he entered the bathroom. He held the jar of beetle cream.

"Oh no. Not again, Wren."

Putting a small dollop on his finger, Wren held it up and asked, "Are you sure, Templar? Can you say with absolute certainty you'll be able to perform after you drop to your knees and take the master's member into your mouth? Remember, you won't be the only one punished if you don't meet the master's expectations."

To his everlasting shame, Nels whispered, "Do it." As Wren applied the ointment, Nels looked into the mirror to see a flame-red blush staining his face. When Wren turned to wash his hands, Nels slipped the trousers on and let Mohammed lead him to the master. He started when he found Abdullah lurking at the top of the tower steps.

Maybe Wren had been right to make him use the cream if the master had invited Mohammed and Abdullah to be present for his initiation. He'd already discovered he couldn't perform in public without a little help from a squashed beetle or two.

He stifled his sigh of relief when his escorts stopped in the outer office and gestured for him to continue into the alcove dominated by the king-sized bed. As if he needed the clue. The master lounged, nude on top of the sheets.

Nels took note of the missing, happy-to-see-you expression on the master's face, dropped his eyes, and wished he hadn't. The master's dick gave the impression of anger as well.

It took him two tries to raise his eyes and force the words he'd been taught through his clenched teeth, "May I pleasure you, Master?"

"Has my little Wren taught you nothing, Templar? You dare to raise your eyes to mine like an equal? Take your trousers off and turn around."

Nels clamped down on his initial reaction to resist and followed the master's command. With his back to the Master, he heard the slither of his body moving across the sheets. And yelped when the Master

grabbed his hair from behind, and twisted him around
to toss him, face first, onto the bed. The master
clutched his waist so hard, he grunted in pain and
went to his knees to get away from the assault.
Primitive instinct took over when he felt the hard cock
poke him in the ass.

With a roar, Nels flipped over and struck out. The
man must've been expecting it because he evaded the
roundhouse swing.

"Do you think me unintelligent, Templar? Now,
you will assume the position, or I'll make you do it
with Mohammed's gun pressed to your temple, and
then I'll let Abdullah take Wren as many times as he
wants."

Trembling, Nels climbed back to his knees and
lowered his head to the mattress. While he didn't care
whether the master shot him or not—well, yeah, he did
care, because he preferred a swift death to a lifetime of
abuse— he didn't want to go to his grave knowing he'd
been responsible for Wren's torture.

The master demonstrated his disdain of small
talk, or kissing, in his preference for immediate
penetration. Nels disobeyed Wren's foremost directive
and clenched in fear. Ahh, shit, it hurt like hell. The
master didn't give him a moment to recover, but

slammed into him accompanied by the slap of flesh on flesh, harsh breathing, and whimpers of pain he was helpless to stop.

Nels thought his pain complete until the master reached around him and grabbed his dick and began working that just as roughly.

"Say it, Templar. Say my name as you come, and I won't take you again this morning, although I should to teach you a lesson. You are nothing more to me than Wren is. You are both my possessions, and I can amuse myself with you until I am tired of you. Do you know what I do with my toys when they no longer interest me? I break them and throw them away. Now, say it. Shout my name, Templar."

Nels would never know whether he complied for the fear of another session with the master or whether the aphrodisiac circumvented his natural resistance, but he performed as ordered, and roared the only name he knew, *Master*.

His capitulation triggered his captor's ejaculation, and he fell to the mattress under the weight of the master's body. He must've passed out for a brief moment because he didn't remember closing his eyes. Mohammed prodded his shoulder and woke him. The sound of running water told him where the master had gone.

Nels stumbled up the tower stairs. He'd been too spent to even dress himself, but his fear came back when he opened the door to find Abdullah standing inside. What in the hell had that bastard been doing in their room? The question immediately called the panic back. He'd just been treated so harshly, it couldn't have been considered anything but punishment. Had he sent Abdullah to punish Wren as well?

Mohammed shoved him roughly into the room as Abdullah stepped out. The door slammed shut, and he heard the lock engage behind him before he could voice a single syllable.

The smell of sex and blood assaulted his nostrils as Nels moved farther into the room. The utter stillness made fear force a cry from his throat. *"Wren!"*

He spotted Wren, facedown and unmoving, on the ruin of the bed. His braid had been wound around his throat, and his beautiful face bruised by open-handed slaps. The blood on the boy's back and legs concerned him the most. The bastard had not been gentle with the delicate Wren.

He held his breath as he waited to see if Wren was unconscious or dead. A mewl of pain made his lungs start functioning again, and he rushed to the bathroom for wet towels and whatever unguent he could find to ease some pain.

When Wren struggled to unwrap the braid from his throat, Nels gently moved his hands away and unwound it for him. He cursed in Danish when he discovered Abdullah had almost strangled Wren with his own silky locks, guaranteeing Wren would be unable to swallow without pain for the next few days. He would've hushed Wren when he started to speak, but stopped as the man shook his head and rasped, "I want to bathe. Help me into the bath. It will take some of the pain away if I can sit in warm water."

Nels agreed and ran to fill the tub large enough to hold them both. As the water foamed into the basin, he rooted around underneath the sink and through the drawers, searching for whatever might soothe the damage done to Wren. He spotted a cardboard box of Epsom salts and added a generous amount. They were good for bruises and swelling, and, between the two of them, they had enough to need a truck full.

Wren lay unresponsive in his arms as he carried him to the bath and eased him into the water. "Hold onto the side of the tub until I get in, and I'll hold you up so you can lie back and soak," he ordered.

He began to worry at Wren's lack of response

when he had to take the boy's hands and shape them over the tub's rim to hold his head above water before he climbed in and grabbed a bath sponge to begin sponging the worst of Abdullah and the master from their bodies.

He had no medical experience with this kind of trauma, so he didn't know if Abdullah had caused any internal damage. At least the bathwater remained clear and free of blood, and he thanked the few Norse deities he could recall from his mythology classes.

Nels didn't want to rouse him when the water turned tepid, but it wouldn't do to let him catch a chill. He pulled Wren to the side of the wide tub and, once again, shaped his unresisting fingers over the rim so he could get out and dry himself off before seeing to his fellow prisoner. As he carried Wren back to the bed, he stopped in consternation and cursed Abdullah for being a sadistic monster. He couldn't bring himself to lay Wren on sheets covered in blood and semen, so he carried him to the one chaise in the room.

"Rest here a minute. I'm going to take the sheets off and use our blankets to cover the mattress until the Oompa Loompas can bring us clean linens."

Not receiving an answer, he peered closely at his charge, and, after verifying Wren still had a pulse, left him to sleep some of his exhaustion and pain away. At least, now he'd be able to pat him dry without causing him anymore pain.

Nels threw the balled up sheets as far from himself as he could, but assumed a rigid stance when he heard the key in the door. They'd have to kill him now, if the master, Abdullah, or Mohammed wanted anything more from either one of them this day.

Nels relaxed when the Oompas walked into the room with their usual avoidance of eye contact. He watched in silence as they made up the bed and uncovered the dishes they'd brought for the last meal of the day. He jerked in surprise when one of them faced him and made a guttural sound.

Not understanding, Nels shouted, "What? I don't understand you. Speak up, for God's sake." He tried to shake off the contact as one of them grabbed his hand, until the man tilted his head back and opened his mouth.

Nels almost emptied the bile he'd carried in his stomach since he entered the master's room at the ugly proof the man's tongue had been removed. The Oompas never spoke to them because they were incapable of speech. Nels fell to his knees and wept. After the Oompas carried Wren to the freshly made bed, the one who'd enlightened him patted him on the shoulder and gestured for him to feed Wren by hand. The Oompas left the room with the nasty sound of the lock engaging once again.

A thready voice had him spinning toward the bed.

"I didn't know their tongues had been removed, either. Now I'm reviewing all of the times I made fun of them, and it has added another layer of hurt."

Nels approached the bed and knelt beside it. When Wren patted the mattress, he climbed on and stretched his body out next to the boy. He only meant to soothe, but when he caressed his cheek, Wren erupted in racking sobs.

"What did I ever do so wrong in the eighteen years of my existence to never have anyone who loves me for just me and not what I can do with my body? Will I ever have anyone who loves me without giving me pain in return?"

Nels closed his eyes in the face of such agony and answered as honestly could. "You've done nothing wrong, Wren. Sometimes a bad thing happens to a good person. Is it God's retribution? I can't bring myself to believe so. You're an innocent. You haven't had the freedom to make bad choices. Those have all been made for you."

When Wren continued to cry as if his heart had been dissolved, Nels put his arm over the boy's chest and his lips next to his ear. "Let me tell you a secret Wren. I have an American friend. His name is Ross, and he's an expert at finding things, and I know he'll find us."

The bitterness crept through the hoarseness of Wren's voice. "What good would that do me, Templar? He'll take you away and I'll be left here."

Nels ran his thumb over Wren's delicately arched eyebrow as he responded. "No, you won't. You'll come with me and I'll get you back to your parents, I swear it."

Rather than reassure the boy, his response made him sob all the harder.

"You don't understand, Templar. I have no one. I thought the master loved me, and now he's treated me worse than one of those Styrofoam cups you toss into the trash when they've served their purpose."

Nels quailed at the response. Wren's situation was so much worse than he'd understood.

"Before you came, I already suspected my time with the master might end soon because I knew he preferred young boys, and when my beard came in, I grew more afraid he'd replace me. When he brought

157

you here, it gave me hope. Maybe, his tastes had changed and I could continue to please him in a different way. But he's just shown me how wrong I was to think so. He said he wouldn't punish me if I taught you how to please him, but he's shown me in a very brutal way I'm nothing but a foolish, caged bird who ignored the bars keeping him captive.

"So, don't offer me false hope, Templar. If your friend does come, I know what my fate will be. He'll take you away, and I'll be sold to someone else when the master tires of me. Wren stabbed Nels in the chest with his index finger, but without much force behind it. "I'm not ever going to love or hope again, Templar, it's just too fucking painful."

Nels swiped his hand across his face to keep his tears from mingling with Wren's. "No, I won't let you give up. I love you, and I won't let you remain here to be abused by the master or anyone else. When Ross comes, you'll come with me, and I'll take care of you for as long as you want or need me. Even though I've known you a short time, I love you, Wren. You've got to believe me when I say love you."

Wren swiped at his cheeks, but the tears continued to flow.

"Once we're free, you won't ever need to take my

body or have me take yours to know so. I love you because you are *you* and there's no one else like you, and I hope you'll love me back for the same reason."

"Do you swear it?"

"On my oath. Come, now. The Oompa Loompas have brought a nice broth. It should soothe your throat. Let me feed you."

Nels almost jumped from the bed for a victory dance when the forlorn bird, whose wings had been clipped, closed his eyes and opened his mouth.

When Wren could eat no more, he lay beside him and waited until the boy's breathing evened out in sleep. He didn't think he'd be able to sleep this night, despite his exhaustion. His conscience bothered him. He'd meant to soothe Wren's pain by telling him of Ross, but had he been inadvertently crueler than the Master by giving him false hope? He didn't know. When it came right down to it, maybe he'd been cruel to himself as well, to believe in a rescue that might never come.

***

Ross wished he'd never suggested they stay a little bit longer to check on Nels after they'd finished their site reconnaissance. As it turned out, the palm grove he'd chosen for his own surveillance had been the best place to cover Otter as he booby-trapped Rashid's vehicle.

Now he and Gunner lay hidden in the *wadi* beneath the tower, and had heard Wren's heartbreaking cries of despair. He didn't know if he'd made a sound or not, but Gunner's pat on his back cleared the black rage from his eyes.

"It will be a pleasure to waste everyone in there who's done anything to hurt your friend and the boy," Gunner vowed, "But the honor of killing Farrid goes to you, Lassie, no one else. I'll tell the rest of the team. Come on, we need to get back and kick the planning into high gear."

Ross kept his eyes on the tower window as he gathered up his listening devices and gave his solemn, silent promise. "You'll not be left behind, Wren. On my honor, you will not be left behind."

# Chapter Twelve

The first glimpse of Prince al-Harbi's security man put Troll's team at ease. If Ross had to guess the man's breakfast choice, it would be nails. The man looked like he could chew a bar of steel and spit out nails. His cheery, English-accented, "Good morning, gentlemen," started the brief off on a positive note, for Suliman, as he'd introduced himself, had been a real concern. The whole plan revolved around the man being competent enough to handle the shooting sequence they'd hashed out this morning.

The balloon went up in two hours, and the thought of having the operation fail because the lynchpin didn't have the requisite experience had kept Ross's stomach in a knot. One look at Suliman, and he eased up. Suliman wouldn't need to have anything spelled out more than once. A little wet work wouldn't phase Prince al-Harbi's man.

Troll began the brief by asking, "Suliman, do you know what Farrid, Abdullah, and Mohammed look like?"

"Yes. I've seen all three. I understand there are

two men being held captive in his compound. I would like to see their pictures, if I may?"

Ross handed Suliman one of the pictures he'd snapped of Wren. He made sure to exclude the one of the boy servicing Farrid. He then handed the prince's bodyguard a passport photo of Nels. It'd been necessary to use the passport photo because he hadn't been able to photograph Nels in the compound.

He approved of the way Suliman studied both photos. It told him the man wouldn't be shooting either one by accident.

As Suliman handed the photos back, Troll asked, "Have you brought all the money, or is it a stack of bills over filler?"

Suliman grinned as he leaned down and patted the metal case by his leg. "Oh, the prince doesn't do anything by half measures. It's all there, all two hundred and fifty thousand dollars."

Otter whistled at the sum. "I could buy a big bang for a quarter of a million bucks."

Gunner leaned in to him, "Yes, you could, and if we don't get Rashid al-Tikriti before he has a chance to use what Farrid paid him, so can he. So you have to make damn sure your cheaper, government subsidized bang keeps him from blowing out more than the candles on Prince al-Harbi's birthday cake."

"Won't be a problem unless I get my dress stuck in the bicycle chain and fall off the damned thing."

Ross joined the rest of the team in snickering. The plan entailed all of them going in dressed in traditional Saudi clothing. Otter would be concealed alongside the entrance road to Farrid's compound, and when Rashid's vehicle passed him he'd wait until the bomb-maker entered Farrid's house before riding his bike up to the car and planting his remote-controlled device. He'd then join Gunner at his position in the palm grove to wait for Ross and Suliman. It would be Troll, stationed where Rashid's car would have to pass on the way back to Riyadh, who'd ruin the bomb-maker's day.

Ross would wait with Suliman in a nondescript utility van, and as the bomb maker passed their vehicle on its way out, they'd approach the compound, picking up Gunner and Otter.

Their operation plan had a lot of moving parts, and they all knew Murphy's Law could and would kick in somewhere. If Murphy ran true to form, it'd kick in at the worst possible time.

Ross crossed mental fingers they wouldn't enter Farrid's office to find Nels and the boy called Wren there. He didn't want either one of them shot by accident. But when Troll called, "It's time to mount up," the jitters fled and his nerves calmed. He looked forward to throwing Farrid a *bon voyage* party for his upcoming trip to hell.

It didn't take long before the team took their assigned positions. Ross felt his adrenaline begin flowing when he saw the rooster tail of dust kicked up by an approaching car, and alerted Suliman. "Rashid's on his way out," and they both slouched down to hide their presence in the vehicle.

Ross did a long count to ten to give the bomb-maker time enough to leave the dirt road to the compound and head toward Riyadh and certain death. At least Ross hoped Troll made it certain. There was always the one in a million chance there'd be something wrong with Otter's bomb or the remote control. Nope, not going there, Ross chided himself. Right now, he focused on switching on the van's ignition and moving to where Gunner and Otter could hop into the back of the van for the short ride.

Once he got to Farrid's front door, the team climbed out and arranged their robes to hide the pistols in their shoulder holsters, Suliman handed Ross the metal case full of money. He would serve as the man's lackey for this *tête-à-tête*.

\*\*\*

Suliman stood next to Ross with Gunner and Otter behind them, and receiving the nod, picked up the iron ring and brought it crashing down on the reinforced door of the compound. He didn't have long to wait before Mohammed opened the door. The widening of the man's eyes told him he hadn't expected more than one person.

Suliman snapped at the bodyguard, "Are you going to keep us waiting out here in the heat and the dust? We are expected. I have other duties to perform for Sabir, and standing here isn't going to see them done."

At the mention of the prince's son, Mohammed bowed them in, and gestured for them to follow him to Farrid's office.

Suliman had to bite the inside of his cheek to stifle his amusement as Farrid stood behind his desk wearing the same astonished expression as Mohammed when the four of them trooped into his office. He noted Abdullah was the better trained security guard, as he showed no emotion, but moved to the room's outer edge to accommodate the influx of visitors.

"Sabir has sent me to deliver this money for the payment you will make tomorrow." He gestured at the case Ross held.

His SAS training took in Gunner gaging Abdullah's height as he walked past the man to take up a position a little in front of the big bodyguard, and Otter moving to stand next to Mohammed on the other side of the room. Excellent, both shooters had clear fields of fire in those positions. It remained for him to give the signal.

Farrid forced him to focus once again on Prince al-Harbi's son-in-law when the man used a petulant tone to ask if it had been necessary to bring so many men to deliver one briefcase.

Suliman bowed slightly, but not in deference to the abomination in front of him. "Sabir thought it necessary to send a security detail. After all, a quarter of a million dollars isn't to be scoffed at, and Suliman swung his gaze around the room and added, "Your compound is in an isolated location"

Farrid appeared not to like his observation. "Fine, you've delivered the money without mishap. You may have your man put in on my desk and your duty is done."

Suliman knew if he obeyed Farrid's order, the

operation would not go as rehearsed. Gunner and Otter waited for the click of the briefcase being opened as their signal to take out Farrid's security men.

Knowing his SAS instructors would be proud of him, Suliman improvised on the spot. "I will leave as soon as you've verified the delivery. I'm sorry, Sabir insists I receive a receipt for what I'm delivering, after you've seen the money."

Not giving Farrid any chance to refuse, Suliman gestured for Ross to step to the desk. With no show of emotion, Ross placed the briefcase on the desk and turned it so Farrid would have a good view of the money when it opened. Knowing Gunner and Otter were in position, he didn't hesitate but reached across the case and clicked open the double latches.

Ross knew the loud bang following a millisecond after the click had been Otter taking out Mohammed with a well-placed shot behind his ear. Ross didn't even flinch at the sound. His concentration centered on the sick fuck who'd held his friend and a young man captive for his sexual pleasure.

When Farrid reared back in shock, Ross put a bullet in the middle of his forehead. He heard Abdullah's shout of "Gun!" from a distance, but he relied on Gunner to do what he did best. Gunner didn't disappoint him.

Abdullah moved when Ross raised his gun, but he never made it to his weapon. Gunner took him out with a head shot and silence reigned in the room, until Suliman coughed at the accumulated cordite, and, in British understatement, said, "Well, this went well. I didn't get a spot on me."

Ross couldn't say the same for himself or the office walls. Having already noted the bedroom alcove, he stepped into the bathroom and returned with a clean face and wet towels. "Here, wash yourselves up, I don't want anyone to scare Nels and Wren when I bring them down."

"Hey, where'd Suliman go?"

Otter wiped his hands on a towel. "He's checking the remainder of this floor to make sure there aren't any surprises before we bring the hostages down."

They didn't have to wait long before the prince's bodyguard returned, herding two cowering men in front of him. "This floor is clean, except for these two. I can't get them to do anything but spout gibberish."

Ross identified them. "They're the house servants. They can't talk because their tongues have been removed. I don't know if Farrid was the one who had it done or not."

One of the Oompa Loompas walked up to Abdullah's body, kicked the corpse and spat on it, and then dropped to the floor with his hands covering his head at the sight of four guns trained on him. The other man chose not to move at all but did raise his hands over his head.

Gunner's laconic, "Well, there's a clue for you," almost startled a bark of laughter from Ross.

Suliman gestured for the two men to take seats on the chaises and handed a key to Ross. "I'm assuming this unlocks the door to your friend's room." He pointed back at the servants, "They seemed most anxious I have it."

Ross asked, "What will you do with them?"

"They are now under Prince al-Harbi's protection. They'll be well cared for. Go and get your friend and the boy. I'll meet you out in the hall. I don't think you should bring them into this room."

Taking in the carnage, Ross couldn't agree more. He turned to Gunner and Otter. "I think it best if I go up alone and bring them down. I don't know how much of the noise they heard, or if they recognized it as gunfire. If they did, they'll be frightened."

Otter patted him on the back and headed for the door. "I'll get the van started. The sooner we get out of

169

here, the sooner I can see if Rashid has been splattered from here to Riyadh. I'm sure Troll is anxious for us to pick him up on the way out. It's past his drinkie-poo time."

Ross took the tower stairs two at a time, but, when he got to the door, he hesitated. Better to follow hostage protocol than barge in. It would be rotten luck if he got shot because Farrid had had someone they didn't know about stationed in the room.

He drew his weapon before he knocked and called out, "Nels, it's me, Ross. I'm going to open the door. I want you and Wren to lie facedown on the floor with your hands locked behind your heads until I tell you you can move. Do you understand?" His heart thumped harder in his chest when he heard, "Yes. Oh God, yes."

Since Nels and Wren complied with his instructions, they couldn't see his jaw drop at the two naked asses staring up at him when he entered the room. Neither man had a stitch of clothing on.

Ross had to force the words out. "Okay, please remain still, I need to check out the room. I'll make it fast. I promise."

He made a quick, but thorough, search of the main room and bathroom then holstered his weapon before telling the men to they could get up. Nels leapt up and almost bowled him over when he grabbed him in a bear hug.

"Oh God, you came. I told Wren you'd come for us, and you did."

Ross patted his back until he stopped shaking. "Let's get you dressed and out of here."

His plan changed when the boy, who'd been standing silently to the side, spoke. "We aren't permitted clothes."

Ross bit his tongue to keep the expletive from escaping. The long-range camera hadn't done justice to Wren. Had he chosen to be a model, the camera would love him. Even with a bruised face and throat, Wren was drop-dead handsome. He held out his hand to the boy and almost cursed again when Wren flinched at his sudden gesture.

Ross gentled his voice. "Hello, Wren. My name's Ross de Lassy. I hope Nels told you I'm his friend, and my friends and I have come to take you out of here. Don't worry about the clothes. We'll, um, borrow some from Farrid."

"I'm sorry, sir. I don't know who Farrid is?"

"Farrid is the one who owned this house." Ross thought he'd have to start changing the subject at this point. He didn't want to have to explain why Farrid wouldn't be needing clothes ever again, but he didn't have to. The look Wren flashed Nels told him the boy was agile at deciphering clues.

Ross continued. "Wait here while I fetch some clothes. Please don't leave this room. There are four of us here, and I don't want anyone to mistake you for a bad person. I'll return very quickly, I promise."

Gunner met him at the bottom of the steps. "What's up? Why haven't you brought them down? Are they okay, or do they need help walking?"

"They're fine, but Farrid wouldn't let them have any clothes. I'm going to have to raid the bastard's closet to clothe them."

Gunner's cursing didn't stop the whole time they pulled whatever they thought they'd need from Farrid's closet. It soon became evident they had no knowledge of Saudi dress, and Suliman pushed them away to select two complete outfits.

He stopped Ross right before he started up the steps. "The money is for the boy. The prince knows it can never repay him for what Farrid did to him, but it should give him a good start in his new life."

For all the bad characters they ran into, sometimes it was hard to remember those like the prince, whose sense of justice insisted the wrong done to Wren by a member of his family be righted as best he could. It gave Ross some faith in mankind and he accepted the money from Suliman.

As Suliman handed over the money he continued, "As you know, I won't be returning to Riyadh with you. You can take the van, and I'll use one of Farrid's cars when I've finished up here. Leave the van at the terminal, and someone will fetch it later. I'm staying to ensure there's no incriminating evidence to tie what we did here to the prince's name."

Ross nodded.

Suliman drew a sharp, curved dagger from his belt and added, "I'm also to ensure Farrid and his two guards never enter Paradise."

He meant the bodies would be mutilated. You couldn't enjoy women in Paradise without your pecker.

Ross returned with Gunner to find Nels and Wren seated on the bed. His gut cramped at how apathetic both men appeared, but shock played a part. Maybe getting dressed and seeing this place in the rearview mirror would help.

"Here you go," he said in an upbeat tone. "The clothes I promised."

Wren turned his head into Nels's chest, as if to hide, and Ross remembered he hadn't entered alone. "Ah, this is my friend Gunner, here to help you get ready, Wren. He won't hurt you. Once you're dressed, we can leave this place."

He had to hand it to Gunner. The man approached the bed as carefully as if he had to cajole a feral critter. The shooter knelt and held up the first garment for Wren's inspection. "I'll be your personal valet, Wren. Let's get you dressed. I'll try not to cause you any discomfort. I'm not sure what goes on first. Is it this one?" Gunner held up the thawb or long dress-like garment."

Ross let out the breath he held when Wren lifted his head from Nels's shoulder and giggled, pointing to another piece of clothing. "No, sir. It's this one, first, and then that one."

As Gunner continued to sweet-talk the boy into donning clothes, Nels dressed himself in record time. Dressed in all white, with the gold-trimmed *mishlah* or outer cloak, Nels could've passed for the English actor who played Lawrence of Arabia. The white-blond hair and beard, and the startling effect of kohl-rimmed, crystal-blue eyes mesmerized him, and his brain sputtered to a standstill. He didn't have any descriptive adjectives left.

Gunner saved him from saying anything stupid. He suggested, since Nels and Wren couldn't pass for Saudis, they should use the tails of their headdresses to cover their faces while traveling.

Ross almost bumped into Wren when the young man hesitated on the threshold to look back into the room. "Is there something you want, Wren?"

"Yes, sir. I'd like to take the pictures Templar drew of me, and a book, if I may?"

"Call me Ross. You can take those. I wish we could take all of your books, but it isn't possible. We'll replace whatever you have to leave behind when we're back in the States.

"Thank you. There's nothing else I want or need to take from here." The boy ran to the sketchpad and scooped it and a thick volume off the floor then exited his former prison without another backward glance.

Outside, Gunner opened the door to the van and leaned in to Ross to whisper, "I wish I'd gut-shot Abdullah for what he did to that kid."

Ross nodded. "The three of them died too easily to suit me."

Wren paused at the back door of the van. "Sir, um, Ross, do you think I could have a window seat? It's been so long since I've seen anything but the inside of this house, and I'd like to be able to see, to see...."

*Jesus God. I want to go back inside and help Suliman remove Farrid's balls.* Ross cleared his throat, and, after tucking the end of Wren's ghutra into the *igal* or rope-like cord holding the headdress in place, he pointed to the seat behind Otter and Gunner and said, "Of course you can, Wren. Now, in you go. I'll sit in the middle so both you and Nels can have window seats. Both of you, please keep your faces covered while we're driving."

It didn't take long on the road back to Riyadh to spot the spiral of black smoke rising from the wreckage of a vehicle, and the solitary Arab walking toward their van.

Otter snickered. "Do you think the Arab fellow who's got his thumb stuck out for a ride is Troll? Maybe we should pass him by and see if he runs after us."

Ross chuckled. "You can do that, if you want, Otter, but I won't stop him from shooting off a sensitive part of your anatomy when he does catch up to this van."

"And here I thought you'd be up for a laugh. Okay, stopping the vehicle now."

Troll cracked everyone up when he opened the door and hopped into the back cargo area. "So help me God, Otter, if you hadn't stopped, I would've shot you as you went by. Good job, by the way. I hung around long enough to make sure nothing slithered from the SUV. I don't think even what little remains of the vehicle will still be there by this evening. People are coming out of nowhere to scavenge whatever they can."

Reaching over the seat to tap Ross on the shoulder, Troll continued, "Why don't you introduce me to your friends, Lassie?"

When they'd stopped to pick up Troll, Ross had made a Herculean effort to remain calm when Wren and Nels each grabbed one of his hands. Now he gave them a slight squeeze and did as Troll requested. "You may remove your face coverings for a moment so I can introduce you. Wren, this is my friend, Captain Trollinger. We call him Troll because he's so ugly he has to live under a bridge, but don't be afraid, he's harmless. And, Troll, this is my friend Nels."

When Nels uncovered his face, Troll whistled. "Whoa, has anyone ever told you, you're the spitting image of that English actor who played Lawrence of Arabia?"

"I don't believe so," came Nels's clipped English voice.

"Look like him and sound like him, you do. C'mon, Otter, crank this muth...er, vehicle up. We've got a plane to catch."

Thanks to Jack Adams's magic wand, all airport and diplomatic hurdles disappeared, and they got clearance to take the van all the way inside the airfield where a chartered 727 awaited them. Ross hesitated at the threshold of first class to find Jack occupying one of the seats after they ditched the van and boarded the aircraft.

After making sure Wren and Nels were belted in for the long flight, he went forward to talk to him.

"I want to thank you, Jack, for letting me go along on the mission. I doubt I'll be darkening your door again."

"I wish I could be sure of that, but you're welcome."

"Why are you on the plane?" he asked. "I thought you'd be kicking back at some fancy restaurant enjoying the fact your rash has started to disappear."

"I'm here to debrief all of you, and to get the ball rolling on helping Wren out. We're going to need some basic information from him, like his real name, where he lived before Farrid bought him, who his parents are. Also, I'm here to make sure the Saudi customs agents, who'll clear this plane, don't find anything to delay us."

Jack handed Ross two passports, one US and the other Danish.

Flipping open the US one, Ross studied Wren's picture. The headshot had been altered by Jack's shop to give the boy a traditional haircut. The kohl-rimmed eyes had been replaced with unadorned ones. But Ross had major heartburn with the surname on Wren's passport, and he gave Jack Adams a what-the-fuck look.

"I see you've read the last name on Wren's passport. I thought about letting him use Kirkegaard, but Nels is a Danish citizen, and Wren's birthplace is the United States. Hope you don't mind the expropriation of your last name and address, Ross. I would've used mine, but my wife might wonder why we suddenly had an eighteen-year-old son she hadn't given birth to, and she's got a bit of an anger management problem. I'd wake up one morning minus my balls if she ever thought I'd been playing around behind her back."

"Well I wouldn't want to see your balls twisted off,

so, no, it's fine for now." The flight attendant's announcement to please take seats and fasten seatbelts for departure kept Ross from saying anything else, but he leveled a glare at the CIA agent and promised, "We'll talk more when we've reached altitude."

Nels watched Ross as he moved down the plane's center aisle, and he wanted to pinch himself to make sure he hadn't dreamed of being freed from the master's clutches. The solid feel of Ross's body as he climbed over him to reach his seat gave him the reassurance he craved.

He'd chosen a seat across the aisle from Wren after discovering Ross and Troll's team had the whole plane to themselves. He let Wren have a whole row in case he wanted to sleep during the long flight. Nels, with the experience of frequent flights under his belt, chose an aisle seat for his long legs.

Ross tossed a Danish passport into his lap, and he studied his own image.

"Here, this will get you through customs when we land. I've got one for Wren, too, but it's a US one."

Nels couldn't seem to get his tongue working again after he murmured his thanks. He'd shut down, not because he hadn't anything to say, but because his tongue had twisted itself into a knot with the many things he needed to convey to his rescuers.

Shutting his eyes to block out Ross's worried expression, he listened to the pilot announce they'd been cleared for takeoff, and a tiny bit of his fear left him as the plane began to move. Not until they leveled out over the ocean did a smidgen of courage return, and he opened his eyes to find Ross staring at him.

"Thank you, Ross. Thank you for coming for me. I...."

Ross squeezed his shoulder. "No, stop, I don't need thanking. You and I became friends while we worked on my renovations, Nels. Part of my special forces training is to never leave a friend behind. So you see, it was never a question of if I'd come for you, but when I'd come for you. I'm sorry I didn't get a quicker start. I waited the whole weekend before I started searching for you because I thought you were, um, with, um...."

Nels reached out and took his hand. "No, I wasn't with anyone, more's the pity. Whoever those men were, they grabbed me as I left the book store. It's funny in retrospect, but I'd left there when I did to find a bar in the hopes of getting lucky."

Nels stopped speaking when Gunner popped up over the back of the seat in front of them. "I'm taking Wren up to meet the pilot. He's never seen the inside of a cockpit before, and the pilot okayed it before we took off. Wren also said he wanted to thank Otter for his help, so I'll introduce the two of them. Oops, Wren is way ahead of me."

Troll, falling into the seat in front of him a few minutes later, woke Nels up from a light doze.

"Wow, that kid has some energy. I swear to God, he was trying to get the stewardess's number. That's one, handsome boy."

Troll's remark sparked something in Nels he wouldn't have been able to explain to anyone who hadn't been privileged to know Wren. "Don't mistake his exuberance for youth. He may look young, but when it comes to all things sexual, Wren is older than any man aboard this plane. It's going to be very difficult equalizing what Wren needs to know to exist within the standards of normal society with what he's been taught by Farrid. I pray his parents or guardians are up to the task."

Looking duly chastised, Troll changed the subject. "Ah, the pilot told me we're out of Saudi Arabian airspace and can now drink without offending religious Muslims. Can I get you something to drink?"

Recognizing the offer for the apology it was, Nels kicked himself for his sharp tongue. "Thanks, Troll. Perhaps you or one of your team can ensure our curious Wren doesn't sample too much liquor. I know he isn't legally old enough to drink, but, just this once, he should be allowed some for medicinal purposes, or at least a celebratory one."

"You got it, Nels. If it's his first taste of liquor, it'll knock him on his ass and put him to sleep, which would be a good thing. I know he's in some pain from whatever abuse he suffered before we got there, but the kid has pluck. He hasn't complained once. Wren would make a good soldier."

Remembering a nursery rhyme an English au pair girl hired by his parents taught him, Nels chanted to himself, "Tinker, tailor, soldier, sailor...." Wren could be all of those and he'd succeed.

Jack shook Ross awake then Nels. Wren was already watching them all. When he had everyone's attention, Jack spoke in a low voice, "Follow me to the first class section. There are some things we need to discuss."

The plane hadn't been configured for a conference

meeting, so Jack sat, tailor-fashion, in the middle of the aisle as Ross, Nels, and Wren took seats in the first row. "Okay, I need to know certain things if I'm going to expedite Wren's re-introduction to his family." Jack asked, " I need your full name, last known address, and the names of your mother and father."

"No."

Jack, who'd been reading what he'd written on his legal pad, raised his eyes. "Wren, we need the information so we can notify your parents."

"That won't be necessary."

"Okay, but we need your birth name to put on all of the official documentation you'll need to live in the United States."

Wren fidgeted with his hair "I'm sorry, sir, but no such person exists anymore. Can't I continue to call myself Wren?"

"Sorry, Wren, but you'll need a last name. To my knowledge, singers and movie stars go by one name, a stage name, but they use their real names on legal documents."

Ross watched the interplay in silence.

The boy had been kidnapped and sold as a sex slave at the age of eleven, so Ross would bet a year's income there were no criminal wants and warrants out for whatever Wren's name had been. Even if he had a juvenile record, it'd be sealed. Serving seven years as a captive sex slave should count as time served, if he'd escaped from a juvenile detention facility.

Wren's answer, when it finally came, was very low. "My name *was* Colin MacAulay. I lived in Denver. My father grew pot. My mother often said, my dad could grow food in a desert but was piss poor at anything else."

Ross could feel the waves of anguish, but he didn't want to interrupt Wren...Colin and maybe stop him.

"He rigged our electrical system to steal from our neighbors, but I guess something must've short-circuited, and my dad, and our house, went up in a puff of fragrant smoke. My mom had driven to the 7-Eleven to pick up a pack of cigarettes right before it happened, or we wouldn't have had any place to live once our home went up in flames."

When Nels tried to offer a word of sympathy, Wren swept his hand down in a violent gesture. "No, don't interrupt me. You wanted to know who I am, and where I came from, and you'll get the whole story.

"My mother smoked pot like my dad. Once we lost the house, she lost whatever restraint she had, and didn't care about anything except scoring more drugs.

185

She left me pretty much on my own, and I became good at stealing from my classmates' pockets, so I could have enough money for breakfast and dinner on the weekends, but some days I went hungry. My mom used our welfare money to buy drugs rather than food."

"I liked school, and not just because it gave me someplace to be away from my mother for most of the day. In fact, I got straight As. I also got good at stealing money from kids too rich to care about keeping track of their wallets. I needed it to do laundry. I never liked being dirty. The shabby part I couldn't help, but I hated showing up to school dirty.

"My mother took care of her appearance as well. Not because she cared, but no man wanted to pay for a skanky looking woman, and she needed the clients to buy her next hit when she ran out of the welfare money.

Wren turned his head away, and his voice got raspy as he continued. "She tried to get me to, to...um.... I told her if she tried to coerce me into turning tricks, she she'd find herself in jail for child abuse and neglect because I'd turn her ass in myself."

Ross stopped himself just in time from punching the window next to him. Wren's tale of parental abuse made him want to find his mother and throttle her.

"You wouldn't think our lives could get much worse, but they did. My mom hadn't scored any money for two weeks because, thanks to her drug use her she looked awful." Wren cleared his throat and stared out the window. "I hadn't been able to steal enough money at school, so we didn't have any money to put gas in the car so we could use the heater. I guess I must've whined once too often that night because my mother came unglued. She said she knew how we could both get what we wanted. A hot meal for me and some primo coke for herself."

Now Ross wanted to punch out every one of Wren's teachers who seemingly ignored all of the signs of a child in distress.

"I should've known something bad was going to happen when, after walking about a mile to a neighborhood I'd never have gone into alone, she introduced me to a friend of hers. My mother didn't have any friends except coke, meth, heroine, or pain pills. But she hadn't lied. I did get my hot meal, and she got the purest shot of coke she'd ever had in her life. She died as soon as she left me there and pushed the plunger of the needle. She'd sold me to a sex ring for one damned shot of oblivion, and both of us died that night."

Ross now wanted to kill or at least maim everyone who'd put this kid in harm's way.

Wren put his head in his hands as a sob tore from his throat. "Goddamn you all for making me relive what I've spent seven years trying to forget. I swore I would never think of it again."

Nels reached over and gathered the sobbing boy into his arms.

Ross swore. "Jesus, Jack. This boy's life has been nothing but one tragedy after another."

"Yes it has." Leaning forward, Jack patted Wren on the shoulder. "But you're no longer a boy, are you? At eighteen, you're a legal adult, and I can't compel you to accept any help I might offer."

Ross burst out, "Well you can't just toss him into mainstream life. This kid has been living in a world with no television, no Internet, no current events, and no contact with the opposite sex for seven years." He slammed his fist into the armrest. "Christ, Jack, it'd be like releasing a convict after serving a thirty-year sentence. If you cast Wren into modern society without any safety nets, you'll be putting him right back in hell."

Jack picked up the legal pad and clicked open his

ballpoint pen. "And what would you suggest I do? Tell me, and I'll write it down right here, right now, and act on it as soon as this plane lands."

Ross got up from his seat to kneel down in front of Wren. He patted Wren's knee until he stopped crying. "Wren, my last name and home address have been put on your passport so we can enter the United States. How about we make that information factual, instead of a legal convenience? I'd consider it an honor to be your legal guardian. Your name would be Wren de Lassy from now on, and you'd live with me until you feel ready to have your own place."

Wren swung his gaze from Ross to Nels in a silent plea for advice.

Nels nodded in Ross's direction. "He's a good man, Wren. An honest man. If he gives you his word, he keeps it."

Jack matched smiles with Ross and Nels when Wren extended his hand to Ross and they shook. That bastard Jack loved it when he played his cards right. Ross suggested Nels take Wren back to his seat and leveled a calculating eye on Jack.

"I didn't miss your cat gorging on a canary expression, Jack. You played me. You knew I wouldn't let Wren be cast out again. Truth is, I'm happy to help, but our mutual Uncle Sam will help as well. It should be a breeze for your agency. After all, the WITSEC program creates new identities with appropriate documentation all the time."

"I think we can—" Jack began, but Ross cut him off.

"I want Wren to have a high school diploma with a good enough grade average to get into college, a social security card, a valid passport, and a legal document showing a name change from Colin MacAulay to Wren de Lassy. Uncle Sam will also foot the bill for any immediate health care and psychological counseling he will need, as well as tuition costs for any future college or technical institution he chooses to attend. And, while we're at it, throw in a stipend to cover clothing and modest entertainment expenses."

Jack made a weak protest. "About the only thing you've left out is reimbursement for yourself. Sounds like our uncle is paying for everything."

Ross gave him a piercing look before answering. "No, he's not. He won't be paying for the security of a stable home, for the guidance I'll give him in making mature choices, and for the reassurance someone truly cares for him without him having to use his body to get it. You can't put a price on those, and I wouldn't accept

it even if you could. Prince al-Harbi also ordered
Suliman to give the bomb maker's fee to Wren, and I
intend to invest it for him so he has a solid nest egg
when he's stable enough to stand on his own two feet."

"And if I say no can do, what then, de Lassy? Will
you throw him to the wolves?"

"Oh, don't even try and play hardball with me.
Unlike the house servants Farrid kept, Wren's tongue
has not been removed. I'm very sure Prince al-Harbi
will be most diplomatically displeased to read his
titillating tale of being held as a sex slave by the
prince's son-in-law in a scandal rag of my choosing."

"Done." And it was done.

# Chapter Thirteen

Ross had no idea how he stayed awake long enough to drive the government loaner from Andrews Air Force Base, where their chartered plane landed, back to his place. All three of them were exhausted from the long trip and heavy emotions that'd tagged along for the ride after the rescue. He could've used someone to talk to, to keep him awake, but Wren and Nels slept the sleep of total exhaustion, and he didn't want to disturb them by turning the radio on.

By the time he reached home, he didn't have the strength to carry two adult men up the stairs to his living quarters, so wake them he did. At least the late hour made it unlikely the few residents of his street would notice men in Arabic dress entering his house.

Once inside, Mr. Murphy showed his ugly mug over the question of who would sleep where. "Oh damn, Nels. We're one bed short since the renovations haven't reached the second guest room. We can let Wren use my bed, and I'll sleep on the sofa in my study."

He didn't receive any arguments from Nels or

Wren, which was a good thing because he didn't have the energy for it. Ross offered a brief good night, shucked his clothes, and fell onto the sofa. He didn't even search for a comfortable position, before, *bam*, lights out.

Ross came awake with the warm and fuzzy feeling of being stroked. He groaned in pleasure until his brain zinged him with the comment, *Feels good, doesn't it? Funny, but for a change, it's not your hand doing the stroking*. Instant rage at being molested in his sleep catapulted him from the sofa with a roar. He knocked Wren ass over heels from the side of the sofa in his haste to get away.

"*Wren*, for God's sake, what are you doing?"

"I'm pleasuring you, Master. You signed for me on the plane, and I'm yours, now."

Ross did a fast count to ten before he picked a nude Wren up from the floor and sat him on the sofa. "Okay, first things first. I am not now, nor will I ever be your master. You are your own master. My name is Ross de Lassy, and now we share the same last name. I am your legal guardian which makes you my legal ward. If it's okay with you, think of me as your older brother. I'll never touch your body the way you just touched mine, and you must believe me when I say I have no desire for you to do that to me again."

Ross planned to do a Google search for someone who dealt with sexual abuse, because Wren needed an appointment. asap.

"Are you angry with me, Ross?"

"Look me in the eye when you ask a question. Men look each other in the eye. No, I am not angry with you." Ross sat down and gave him a light fist rap to the shoulder. "I realize you need to establish boundaries of what you can and can't do, and I do know it'll be trial and error at first, so don't worry about this. Trust me, Wren, I'm on your side, and if you do mess something up, we'll talk about it, and I'll give you courses of action on how to fix things."

Wren reached out and ran his hand over Ross's morning beard. "Rough, I like it."

Ross grabbed Wren's hand and placed it back in the boy's lap. "Okaay, I think our first lesson will be learning the difference between honest affection and stone-cold sex. I like you, Wren. I might put my arm around you, give you a hug, maybe even a kiss on the cheek, but I will never, ever engage in sex with you. Same in reverse. You may hug me, lie on the same couch with me, touch me in a non-sexual way, and I'll enjoy it. Servicing me sexually is not acceptable. Are we on the same page here?"

When Wren lowered his head and began to speak, Ross put his finger under his chin until he again had direct eye contact. "I had to try, Ross. People say all sorts of things and do others. I woke up in your house, and in your bed, and I needed to see if you expected me to do more than sleep in it."

"Have I answered your question to your satisfaction, Wren?" Ross had to draw in a breath when Wren leveled a killer grin at him.

"One hundred percent, but I have another question, if I may?"

"Sure, what do you want to know?"

"When's breakfast? I'm starving."

"How's pancakes, bacon, and eggs sound to you?"

"Fantastic. I haven't eaten those foods in seven years. I bet if you included coffee, Nels would join us."

"You know him well."

"Yes, I do, in both the good friend and the Biblical sense, but now I guess it's going to be limited to the good friend sense, huh? Are we playing peek-a-boo, Ross?"

Ross removed his hands from his eyes and answered Wren's question. "Affirmative. I understand what you and Nels had to do keep yourselves alive, but you must realize Nels would never have touched you, otherwise."

"Yes, I do. You were his friend before me, Ross. I know he feels guilty for what he had to do. You need to help him as well."

"I'll do all I can for him."

"Do what?"

Both Wren and he jumped to find Nels standing in the doorway.

Wren covered their discussion of Nels like a pro. "Why lure you out of bed by making a pot of coffee and wafting the aroma in the direction of your room. Ross promised me pancakes and eggs and bacon, and I'm starved."

When Wren stood up and started to stroll toward the kitchen, nude, and in no way self-conscious to be so, Ross went to his dresser, snagged a pair of boxer-briefs, and slung them at him. "Here, put these on. I guess we'll go clothes shopping after breakfast."

***

An hour later, when Nels and Ross prepared to leave the house, Wren protested. "Why can't I go with you?"

"Nels, you want to field that one?" To make his

point, Ross picked up a hank of wavy gold hair from where it flowed down Wren's bare chest.

"I'd be happy to. For one thing, Wren, you haven't any clothes to leave this house. Shopping in the nude is frowned on."

"Okay, but no bow ties."

"No bow ties," Nels agreed.

"I don't want to wear any tie at all. Seeing that tie around your neck makes my throat hurt all over again. Why can't I just wear loose trousers like before?

"Men do not wear see-through pants in America. You need clothes that will make you fit in and not stick out. Now, stand up and let Ross measure you."

Wren obediently held still as Ross measured his neck, chest, waist, and arm length, but the imp surfaced when he tried to measure the inseam.

"I've never had anyone measure my balls before."

"For the love of God, Wren, filter, please. Ross is trying to see how long your legs are. He isn't measuring your balls."

"Sheesh, just kidding, Nels. Wren picked up the remote control for the television and began flipping through the channels. He stopped when a National Geographic special caught his attention, but looked up when Ross suggested maybe Nels should stay home with him.

"What, do you think I'm going to lift my leg and mark my territory on your furniture? I assure you I'm housebroken. I don't need a babysitter. And, yeah, I know, don't answer the door, telephone, or leave the house. If the television bores me, I'll read the book I brought with me. Since we've finished *Macbeth*, I'm looking forward to starting *Midsummer Night's Dream*.

"Well if you haven't finished it before we return, I'll read the parts with you, " Nels offered.

"Thanks, but now please go. It seems strange to say this, but the two of you hovering over me is making my eye twitch. I'll be fine. I'm not planning on swallowing anything, opening a vein, or jumping from any heights. My newfound freedom is too precious to do something that stupid."

Ross wished he could believe Nels wouldn't attempt anything in the self-harm realm, either. He'd seen that look of disconnection before. Indeed, he recognized it well from his own mirror. One too many fire fights, one too many friends lost, but, unlike many others, he'd availed himself of the psychological counseling offered after traumatic incidents.

He knew many soldiers thought it would hurt their military record to do so, but he'd rather be denied promotion than be scarred from things beyond his control. He planned on visiting his psychologist again to talk about his rescue of Nels so he could work through the guilt of not starting his search sooner. He couldn't stop thinking, if he hadn't waited for the entire weekend to pass, he might've found him before Nels had been tortured or had to submit to Farrid.

He opened his mouth to suggest Nels seek some counseling when the other man spoke first.

"Would you mind if, once we get to the mall, I go and get a haircut? I want this beard shaved off as well. I never liked having a hairy face. I can meet you for lunch at the delicatessen at noon."

After parting with Nels, Ross made the circuit of men's clothing stores, and surprised himself when he glanced at his watch as a salesman rang up yet another purchase. Three hours had flown since he and Nels had parted ways, and now, if he hurried, he had enough time to drop the armload of bags off before meeting Nels for lunch. He would've brought them along, but they would take up too much space in a booth. Wren would now be able to go about in public without creating a scandal.

As he turned to leave the store, Ross spotted the shoe department and realized Wren would have to wear the sandals he wore from Saudi Arabia until he could get him into a shoe store to try on shoes.

He jogged his memory again when he stopped to admire a suit on one of the mannequins. Wren would also need a trip to a barber if he didn't want to be singled out for such long hair.

Ross entered the delicatessen more or less on time and spotted Nels in a far booth, and, rather than approach, he stopped to observe him. He could almost feel the pain vibes emanating from Nels who sat totally still, staring down at the table. The Dane's face showed no emotion, and he wasn't paying any attention to what was going on around him, even though the group of women in an adjacent booth were whispering to one another about his handsomeness.

Okay, enough of this. The first lesson was going to be situational awareness. Ross changed directions so he could approach Nels from the rear. He clamped his hand down on Nels's shoulder, and the man almost levitated from the booth.

As he seated himself, Ross said, "That was lesson one, Nels. You need to learn how to look around you.

You made it much too easy for those men to grab you at the bookstore. I didn't enjoy scaring you, but you need to know who's around you, and where the exits are in case something goes wrong and you need to get away. I know I have an unfair advantage because I was taught it in the service, but that doesn't mean civilians shouldn't have their own street smarts."

Pushing a rectangular box across the table, Ross continued, "Here's a small present from me to you. Open it now."

Nels's hands trembled as he reached for the box. "A knife? No one has ever given me a knife for a gift."

Ross reached over and took the large-bladed pocket knife from the box. "You will get used to carrying it. When we get home, I'll show you the proper way of holding it, should you need to use it for something other than slicing apples or cleaning your fingernails. Think of it as just another tool in your toolbox, and it won't make you nervous about using it when you have to."

"I thank you for the gift, Ross. After such generosity, it seems like the wrong time to ask for a favor, but..."

"Whatever it is, you know I'll help, if I can." The waiter chose that moment to come to their booth.

After ordering, Ross waited for Nels to continue, but he just pushed his water glass from side to side and stared at the tabletop.

He reached across and grabbed one of Nels's hands to make him stop. He sucked in a breath when the saddest blue eyes he'd ever seen met his own. "What is it? You can ask me, I won't let you down. Do you want to talk about what happened?"

"No."

"Okay, I understand you might not feel comfortable talking to me, but you should talk this out with a professional."

Nels hissed his disagreement

"There's nothing to be ashamed of in going to a psychologist. I use one myself. I can get you an appointment if you want "

"Thank you, but no. I'm quite capable of working through this on my own."

Ross had his doubts, but kept his opinion to himself and made a strategic retreat from discussion of counseling. "Well, you wanted a favor from me?"

"I want to go back to the bookstore and walk through the alley next to the coffee shop." Nels grimaced, "You might say I want to lay the ghost of my kidnapping to rest."

"Okay, we can do that right after lunch. It's not far from here." Changing the subject, Ross asked, "Describe the people sitting in the booth behind us, and the ones in the booth across from us, and tell me where the exits are in this restaurant."

Nels shook his head. "I don't know. It's impolite to stare."

"Well take a moment to be impolite, and then tell me," Ross demanded in a sharp tone. He waited until Nels checked out the diners and began describing what he'd seen in accurate detail. What an eidetic memory. It gave him a jolt to remember what he'd promised Bernie when he'd begun his search for his friend.

"Nels, I have a favor to ask you when we get to the bookstore. No, I'm not going to ask it now. Let's enjoy our lunch and relax a little."

Nels's throat ached from forcing the corned beef sandwich down. Although he gave the pretense of enjoying lunch, in truth, he'd come close to gagging on each bite. He didn't know how to cope with this sadness. Until his kidnapping, he'd been an optimistic sort and rarely depressed.

Ross's offer of psychological counseling or a shoulder to cry on went against his Danish reserve. He couldn't picture his parents or grandfather spilling their guts to anyone, let alone someone not part of their immediate family. He realized he didn't want to talk to Ross because he didn't want to lose the man's friendship. And he would, if he blurted out how he felt about everything he'd experienced in Farrid's compound, so, *thanks for the offer, Ross, I'll work it out by myself.*

Realizing he hadn't spoken a single word since they'd gotten into the car and driven to the bookstore, Nels steeled his resolve and approached the Jamaican barista. God bless the woman's natural chattiness, for she got the ball rolling.

"Mister Nels, so good to see you again. I see your friend found you. Triple espresso as usual?"

"Yes, thank you. I'd like two, please. My friend here drinks the same thing."

"Oh I remember. I never forget the orders of handsome men, and the two of you brighten any room you walk into. Now have a seat at any table. As you can see, we're not busy, and I'll bring your order when I've finished making it."

When Ross closed his eyes in appreciation of the first sip of the potent brew, Nels had to look away. He'd found the innocent action sexy, and his cock twitched in appreciation. *What the hell?* After Farrid, he didn't think his dick would come out of hibernation for the remainder of his lifetime. Maybe atrophy and drop off, but not twitch at the slightest provocation. *Provocation? Ross coming on to another man? Gaaaah, I'm losing it.*

*After one month of experiencing the Middle East at its worst, my libido's developed a real kink if I can look at someone and have these thoughts.*

Ross missed his mouth and dribbled coffee down his chin when Nels blurted, "The last time I was here, I was reading a book on the Battle of Hastings. Do you know what I discovered?"

"No, but I'm interested in hearing what interests Doctor Kirkegaard," Ross teased.

"Do you know what the Danegeld was?"

"Um, let me think. Wasn't it the tax levied to pay to keep the Vikings from raiding certain parts of England?"

"Excellent, Ross. You know your history, but did you know your hero, William the Conqueror, payed the Danegeld as well?"

"No, I didn't."

"Oh yes. He had his hands full trying to whip those recalcitrant Anglo-Saxons in line to consolidate his power, so he paid the Vikings off to keep them from challenging him until he became strong enough to take them on, but wasn't able to do so during his lifetime. I guess the moral of the story is, we Vikings are a contentious lot, but we can be had for a price."

He grinned when Ross threw his head back and laughed heartily. It felt good to grin about something again. He almost lifted his hand to see if his faced hadn't cracked with the effort.

Taking the last sip of his coffee, Nels stood. Time to face his demons. "Let s take a stroll through the alley, shall we?"

He waited until Ross tossed back the remainder of his drink and followed him to the door. "If you don't mind, let me walk through first, and you can follow. This shouldn't take long. Christ, I don't even know why I'm doing this, but it's something I need to do."

"I understand, Nels. Believe me, I do."

Nels didn't know what he expected would happen, but the narrow passage didn't scare the hell out of him, as he thought it might. Dark, dirty, fetid, but not scary now that Ross accompanied him. Still, he recalled the faces and the strength of the men as they hustled him through it, despite his feeble resistance.

Ross was right. He needed to be more aware of his

surroundings, and he would work on it because it would've given him some small amount of satisfaction if he'd left one or two of them on the ground clutching their balls before he was drugged and thrown into the back cargo area of a van.

As they reached the street, Ross tapped him on the shoulder.

"Nels, could you identify those guys who took you, or recall any detail about the place they kept you? If you can draw it for me, I'd like to take it to an FBI agent I know. The sooner they can shut this ring down, the better. Any little clue at all would be helpful to them."

"Of course. I remember what the men who grabbed me looked like. I can and will draw their faces for your friend. As to the place where they took me, I can sketch the view I had from the window in the closet-sized room they kept me in."

"That would be a start."

"I'm going to be honest and say, while I can sketch it, the drugs they gave me might make it inaccurate. It might be a real view or it might be something my drugged mind thought it saw. I'll get right on it when we get back to your place. Now let's go show Wren his new clothes."

Neither he nor Ross were prepared for the sight of Wren holding his long braid as a welcome back gift when he met them at the door. He'd found a pair of scissors and, securing both ends with a rubber band, hacked it right off.

Ross found his voice, first. "My God, Wren, what possessed you? We should've added no cutting hair to your list of don'ts."

"I grew bored with the National Geographic program and started flipping through the TV channels, and I came across this special about donating hair to cancer victims. There's a beauty salon right here in Alexandria taking donations from anyone who wants to donate, and they'll style your hair for free, if you do so."

Now Nels spoke up. "But, Wren, you took such pride in your hair. Whatever possessed you to cut it? I can still see you brushing it out each morning."

Wren took a step back. "No, I *was* proud of it until Abdullah used it to control me while he raped me. Never again, Templar. No one will ever be able to hold me down by using my hair. I'll never wear it long again."

Nels opened his arms and hugged Wren when he moved into them. The fear he heard in Wren's voice when he mentioned Abdullah, and the use of the name Templar told him he wasn't alone in wrestling with demons.

Squeezing Wren tighter, Nels offered an apology. "You're right. It's your hair, and you can do what you want with it. It's generous of you to donate it to someone who'll be able to use it."

Ross broke the tension by laughing, "Well, I guess we'd better get you over to the salon before the offer ends." He left and returned with a plastic grocery bag. "Here, why don't you put your braid in this?"

Wren rubbed his hand over the back of his exposed neck. "Is there a breeze in here? I had no idea how warm my hair kept my neck and back."

Ross shook his head at Wren's complaint and turned to Nels. "Nels, do you want to accompany us or do you want to be surprised by the new Wren when we return?"

"I'll wait. I'll use the time to begin those sketches you asked for."

Both he and Ross gave appreciative whistles when Wren came out of his bedroom wearing jeans, T-shirt, and sandals. If you ignored the obvious need for a good haircut, Wren could pass for any other normal American male. But, in Wren's case, outer

appearances could be deceiving. He hoped Wren
would someday be able to balance the outer with the in

ner. He desired the same thing for himself.

## Chapter Fourteen

Ross climbed the stairs to the third floor after he returned with Wren. He stood quietly while Nels worked at the large canvas of a forest scene, not wanting to disturb the artist at his work. He didn't think Nels knew he'd entered the room until he spoke.

"How'd the haircut go?"

"It went well. Wren was a big hit. His braid was much prized. You wouldn't believe how different he looks with short hair. It makes his face look more mature. I questioned his desire for hair almost as short as a buzz cut, but it works for him. He must exude pheromones by the barrelful because he had the entire staff, male and female, eating out of his hand by the time we left."

"That's Wren. If he sets his mind to charm, you don't have a chance. I should know."

"Nels, about ...."

"No. I'm not going to discuss that chapter in my life, ever. You'll find the sketches I did on the chaise over there. I hope they help."

Ross crossed the room and opened Nels's sketch book. "Wow, these are good. Probably as good as a black and white mug shot. You really do have a photographic memory."

Nels's began to protest.

Ross held up his hand to stop him. "Yes, I do know the difference between photographic and eidetic, but still, these are fantastic. Wren's requested spaghetti and meatballs for dinner. Will you be able to take a break to join us?'

"No, I feel the need to work more than hunger. Just make a plate up, and I'll grab it when I can. I do know how to work a microwave. Wren taught me."

Feeling dismissed and unaccountably sad for his friend, Ross headed back to the kitchen to cook. He'd made an appointment for Wren to talk to a good psychologist the next day, but he wished he could get Nels to do the same. He could make the suggestion, but it would be up to the Dane to make the move.

*\*\**

Last night's dinner without Nels to serve as a buffer between him and Wren had been a real rollercoaster ride when Wren aimed his curiosity of all things psychological directly at Ross. He almost regretted showing Wren how to use the Internet because he'd used some of his time while he and Nels shopped for his clothes to research topics like drug abuse, child abandonment, pedophilia, and sex trafficking. By the subject of most of Wren's questions, he appeared to be most interested in the concept of the throwaway child.

Ross managed to dam the spate of questions with the pat excuse he wasn't a qualified psychologist, and suggesting he write down the questions he wanted the psychologist to answer during his visit the next day.

Now here he sat in the psychologist's waiting room reading a magazine. Well, giving the appearance of reading a magazine, anyway. He flipped pages at random times but his eyes refused to focus on anything other than the closed door to the psychologist's office. Wren had done a complete 180 this morning and gone from eager to reluctant to keep the appointment with Dr. Anton Lewandowski.

Never having met the psychologist before, Ross hoped he had a strong personality or Wren would enjoy leading him where he wanted him to go. At least he'd reminded Wren in the car on the way to his appointment to be honest when he spoke to the man, or it would be impossible for the doctor to help him recover from his experiences in Saudi Arabia.

Wren calmed down, or at least appeared to, when Ross volunteered he'd sought counseling after traumatic events in his own life.

***

Ross tossed the magazine he hadn't been reading back onto the table when the door opened and Wren shot out like a heat-seeking missile but didn't stop to wait for him.

The psychologist held up his hands in a placating gesture. "Believe it or not, Mr. de Lassy, it went well. Wren has carried a lot of anger around for most of his life, so it will be a slow process to vanquish it. My advice to you, don't smother him with concern. He'll talk to you when he's ready."

Ross remained silent as Doctor Lewandowski verified the waiting room was empty before he spoke.

"Were you in the military, Mr. de Lassy?"

"I was."

"Did you see combat?"

Ross gave the psychologist an affirmative nod. "I did."

"Well then, you are familiar with the symptoms of PTSS. The anger, the panic attacks, the nightmares."

"I most certainly am. I see a psychologist recommended by the VA."

"Excellent, your familiarity with these symptoms will allow you to recognize them in Wren. Has he ever spoken to you about his mother?"

Ross stiffened at the mention of Wren's mother. "Yes, he has. I know she sold him to a sex trafficker for a hit of heroin or cocaine."

"Good, then I won't have to explain to you why Wren suffers from PTSS. Abandoned or throwaway children can suffer the same anxieties as combat veterans. Now, you'd better catch up to Wren before he decides to walk home. I'm not sure he knows the way. Same time next week?"

"Yes, thank you. I'll make sure Wren keeps the appointment." Ross threw down the magazine and ran out to the parking lot to find Wren sitting on the hood of his SUV.

"I don't want to talk about it. You can't make me."

"I would never ask you to tell me what you discussed with the doctor. What goes on behind his closed door is between the two of you. You can tell him anything you want and I'll never be the wiser."

Wren let out a huffing breath and asked, "For real?"

"Yes. I told you I also use a psychologist from time to time, and believe me, I wouldn't want anyone else to know what I discuss. For me it's kind of like a stream-of-consciousness thing. My counselor never offers any quick fixes, but he does ask a question from time to time to get me talking about what I'm feeling. Seems like a waste of money until you realize you do feel better for being able to get it off your chest."

"Do you really feel better?"

"I do. And then there's the added benefit of being able to express things you think make you weird or awful, and knowing it'll go no further than his office. I kind of liken it to being honest with yourself will keep you honest."

Ross relaxed when Wren tilted his head in consideration, and then straightened with a grin breaking over his expressive face. "If Dawg de Lassy can do it, so can I. I guess I'll keep the next appointment."

"Done. Now, how about we head home?"

"Um, before we do, could we do a drive-by through Washington, DC? I've never seen the Washington monument, the White House, or any other of the national landmarks. Denver was too far away to even think about visiting those sites."

"It'd be my pleasure to show them to you, Wren. I'll even go you one better and take you to the Smithsonian Museums tomorrow. Which would you prefer to start with, the Air and Space Museum or Natural History?"

Wren chose the Natural History Museum, and Ross would ensure they covered it from end to end.

His intention to take Wren to the Smithsonian got scrapped the next day, however. He wanted to kick himself for answering the phone right before they got out the door. Now he had to ask Nels to do the honors while he waited for a new client.

When he went to buzz the gentleman in, Wren beat him to it and ushered Mr. Bristol into the office. He knew from talking to the man, Mr. Bristol owned a harness racing stable in Loudoun County. Over the phone, Mr. Bristol had confided his stable, the Fox Trot, had hit a spot of bad luck. First, one of his pacers went lame, then a sulky lost a wheel in the home stretch and almost killed the driver and injured the horse, and, now, a delivery of oats made the horses in his stable sick enough to forfeit a race. Mr. Bristol couldn't explain it, but suspected foul play. The man offered enough money to convince Ross it would be worth his while to go undercover as a stable hand.

"Thanks for seeing me on such short notice, Mr. de Lassy. One of my private investors recommended you to me."

"And who might that have been?"

"J. P. Morgan. He said if anyone could find out the cause of my troubles, you could."

Talk about a small world. When Bristol turned his attention to Wren, Ross made the introductions. "Mr. Bristol, this is my brother, Wren. Wren, I'm going to have to take a rain check on our museum trip. Why don't you see if Nels can take you this morning?"

Ross hoped the speed with which Wren exited the office didn't signify anger, but Mr. Bristol captured his attention again before he could worry about it.

***

The total absence of sound puzzled Nels enough to go in search of Wren. He found him sitting on the sofa in the great room with his head in his hands. "What is it? What's wrong?"

Wren sat up and swiped at his eyes. "Ross can't

take me to the museum this morning. He's interviewing a new client downstairs and suggested you might take me, instead."

"Sure, no problem. Ross will make it up to you another time.

"Shit, Nels, going or not going to a museum isn't the problem. Ross introduced me to his client as his brother. He honestly meant it when he said he thinks of me as a brother. He said he cared for me, but I didn't believe him until now. Going from having no family to having an instant brother caught me off guard. With you being the first exception, I have no experience with people who mean what they say."

Nels sat down and threw an arm around him. "I know what you mean. Until I met Ross, I didn't have much experience, either. You can trust him. If he says he's going to do something, you can take it to the bank." He stood. "Let's get out of here. I don't suppose I can talk you into visiting the National Gallery of Art, instead?"

"No, I want to see the Natural History Museum first. We can visit an art museum second."

Nels gave his shoulder a light fist bump. "Cavemen, dinosaurs, and large, cursed diamonds it is then."

***

Ross flashed a wicked grin at Nels as the Dane dragged himself up the stairs after Wren, who, with the exuberance of youth, had enough energy left to bounce his way to the great room to surf the channels.

"Can I offer you a drink?"

"More like a tank of oxygen. My God, I should be used to his energy by now, but we covered the museum from stem to stern and then he insisted on visiting the National Art Gallery as well.

Ross chuckled.

"My legs are throbbing, my head aches, and I can't, for the life of me, remember one thing I've seen in the five hours we spent going from one room to the next. Would you believe he even managed to meet an attractive girl his own age in the Hope Diamond exhibit? I believe they're meeting for coffee tomorrow. Since you reneged on the museum tour, you get to play chauffeur-chaperone tomorrow."

Ross grimaced. "I have to go undercover starting tomorrow. My new client wants to find out who's sabotaging his racing business. If it'll give you any satisfaction, I'll be shoveling horse shit for the foreseeable future."

"Now if you were to step in it, as well as shovel it, that might assuage my disappointment."

He hated backing out yet again. Nels did look worn out. In fact, the purple shadows under his eyes suggested he hadn't been sleeping well. Feeling guilty for backing out again, Ross offered, "If you can't manage it, I can tell Mr. Bristol he'll have to wait another day or so."

Nels pulled a bar stool away from the kitchen island and sat down. "No, it's fine. Wren needs to mingle with people his own age. He told me the girl goes to George Mason University, and maybe you should look into George Mason as a possible choice for Wren. With his intelligence, Wren should attend a university."

"I'm not sure he's ready."

"I've been tutoring him in spare moments, and I'll bet he'll score high on the SATs. Believe it or not, he's taught himself geometry, algebra, and physics, and he's read all of the classics he can get his hands on. He speaks Arabic, so he's got the language requirement, but he should learn at least one more."

Ross counted the times Nels rubbed the side of his neck and recognized the sign of tension. Not stopping to think, he stepped forward and massaged the man's neck. "Here, let me show you a little something I learned from Tomodashi-san. It's great for relieving kinked muscles."

Ross worked the knots in his neck and shoulders without waiting for permission. He felt his friend relax.

"Ah, you should charge for your services."

"Ha! Tomodashi-san is the one who puts the kinks in the muscles. It's only fair he shows you how to get rid of them."

"You'll have to mop me up from the floor if you continue," Nels complained.

"I've kept dinner warming. Call Wren and we'll eat."

A half hour later, as he and Ross pushed their chairs back from the table, Nels asked, "Am I mistaken or did Wren inhale his meal like a vacuum?"

Ross laughed. "He did, indeed. I'd like to credit the excellence of my veal piccata, but your description is more in line with a growing male's appetite. I do remember this stage. My mother referred to it as trying to fill a bottomless pit."

"Well since you did the cooking, the bottomless pit and I will clean up the kitchen. Wren, turn the TV off and get your ass into the kitchen for cleanup duty."

Nels's use of such an American expression cracked him up, but he didn't hang around to see the result. He had packing to do.

\*\*\*

Ross almost gave a whoop of relief when his cell phone rang and he backed away from the pacer eyeing him like he couldn't decide where to bite him. Putting a tongue tie in a pacer's mouth wasn't easy if the horse had a mind not to cooperate, and this particular horse always extracted his pound of flesh if you weren't quick about it. Mr. Bristol grinned at him when he made the excuse he needed to take the call. His boss knew of Ross's lack of rapport with the high-strung animal.

Ross sat on a bale of hay and slid his thumb across the face of the phone to open the connection. "Ross here."

"Hey it's Wren. Nels had a great suggestion this morning. Why don't you let us work on the other guest room while you're gone? He promised to show me how to use the tools, and he even said I might be able to select the colors and the bed, if you're okay with it. We can keep you in the loop by phone so you'd have final approval."

"Sounds like a plan. So, how did the coffee date go with the girl you met at the museum?"

Wren laughed. "Oh, you mean Sally. It went great, and I'm meeting her again next weekend. She's invited me to her apartment on DuPont Circle for dinner. I've already told Nels he won't have to wait up."

Ross moved the phone away from his ear to stare at it before shaking his head and resuming the conversation. "Okaay, are you sure you're ready for girls, Wren?"

"Don't worry, Ross. I've researched female anatomy on the Internet. I know what goes where and that girls like more foreplay than men. I believe I can adapt my technique to accommodate the differences."

Nels yelled in the background, "For God's sake, Wren. Filter, filter, filter."

Ross took in a relieved breath when Wren giggled and admitted, "Just kidding. Sally has two roommates. I'm going to her place for dinner, nothing more."

"Just be careful."

"Sally's from Iowa and a good girl. Who knows, maybe some of her goodness will rub off on me. Hmm, or maybe we'll rub some body parts together and start a fire. Hanging up, now. Nels is starting to splutter again."

Shaking his head at the whirlwind named Wren, Ross hurried back to help his temporary boss finish attaching all the straps tethering the pacer to the sulky or driving cart. At least the horse turned his attention to strutting his stuff on a track instead of inflicting bodily injury.

It took him three more weeks to find Mr. Bristol's culprit, one of the drivers. The twenty-year-old had a bone to pick with Mr. Bristol by way of unacknowledged paternity. The man's mother had never married Bristol, and, in all fairness to the racing stable owner, never told him he'd fathered a child. She'd forgotten to mention her failure to communicate her pregnancy to Mr. Bristol when she revealed Bristol's identity to her son.

In Ross's opinion, the guy had lucked out when Bristol decided to overlook the mischief and not prosecute, but he'd done what he'd been hired to do, and, now, as he climbed the stairs to his living quarters, he had a single desire. He wanted a long, hot shower and plenty of soap to wash the smell of horse from his skin and hair.

By the time he finished showering, the clock had

bid midnight a fond farewell, and Ross decided to see if either Wren or Nels was still awake. He smiled as he opened the door to Wren's new room, for his ward lay sprawled sideways in his new, king-size bed. Like himself, Wren eschewed clothing when sleeping, as evident by the bare torso and long line of hip and leg not covered by the sheet.

The door to Nels's room was open, the bed vacant. He'd find the Dane on the third floor in his studio, but, when he made the climb, the sight of Nels disturbed him. He'd lost weight in the three weeks Ross had been gone, and even though Nels had fallen asleep on the leather chaise he'd dragged up to his studio, Ross wouldn't have said he looked comfortable.

The artist twitched and moaned, as if his dreams had turned into nightmares. He tried to back up quietly, but his heel hit the door behind him with a distinct clunk, and a curse broke free before he could stifle it. Nels sat straight up with a shout.

"Jesus, I didn't mean to scare you. I came up here to check on you before going to bed. I got home pretty late and had to take a shower or you'd think I'd brought a horse home as a pet." He managed to stop the dithering when Nels gathered himself together and scrubbed his hands over his face.

"Wren will be glad to see you when he wakes. He worked hard on his room, and he shows an aptitude for carpentry, and I had fun working with him. Why don't we go downstairs? I could use something to eat, I forgot dinner tonight."

Ross stopped him with a question. "Why are you pushing yourself so hard? You could use a good night's sleep as well as some grub."

Nels brushed past him without answering.

He had to double-time it down the stairs to catch up to his friend. "What's going on? Is it anything I can help you with?"

Milk splattered all over the counter as Nels slammed the milk carton down. "No, you can't help me unless you have something I can take to knock me out cold for two or three days so I can sleep. Every time I close my eyes, I relive my last encounter with Farrid. I'm a goddamn coward, Ross. I can't sleep because I'm afraid to sleep."

"Let's talk about it—" Ross began.

"No."

Ross mopped up the mess and poured milk into a saucepan. " Perhaps a shot of brandy in it will help."

Nels turned and shuffled off to his room with all the grace of a zombie.

Ross added the liquor and followed him with the cup. "I'm not going to fuck around and give you a bunch of platitudes like oh, you'll work it out for yourself, or, give yourself time to heal. Both you and Wren went through a terrible experience, and you both need professional help to get through this. You're suffering from Post-Traumatic Stress syndrome. Most people associate PTSS with combat, but you don't have to be shot at to get it."

Nels rolled over and hugged him like a drowning man being rescued. "I can't talk about this."

Ross gave his shoulder a squeeze. "I know it's difficult, but psychologists are not judgmental, and whatever you tell them is confidential. Nothing you tell him about what went on with Farrid would make him kick you out of his office."

When he trembled, Ross rubbed circles on his back to calm him, but he found himself being shaken as Nels punctuated each word with forceful tugs. "Even if I told him I fucking enjoyed it? I'll bet you're happy now to have me as a house guest? I fucking enjoyed being fucked by another man."

Ross wrapped his body around the Dane's and held him in his arms until he stopped struggling.

"Listen to me, listen to me. I've been doing some

228

reading on men held in captivity for prolonged periods, and there was a study done on prisoners that said some men keep their real-man identities by seeking sexual release with another male rather than deny themselves. It's a coping mechanism, Nels. You did what you had to do to cope with the belief t you might not ever be free of that life."

Ross continued to run his hand up and down Nels's back until the exhausted man fell asleep.

***

God it felt so good to wake up rested. Nels couldn't remember when his eyes didn't feel like they'd been abraded by sandpaper, or when his muscles weren't knotted in painful kinks. The warm and fuzzy feelings ended when a string of drool escaped his mouth and landed on a bare male chest. He sat up in a rush but calmed when he discovered the chest belonged to Ross, not Farrid. He had spent the entire night with him.

Nels inched to the other side of the wide mattress in increments to avoid waking Ross. How in the hell could he explain to his friend his theory on male prisoners didn't apply to him in the slightest?

Nels turned the shower on and stripped off his T-shirt and jeans. Steeling himself, he braved his reflection in the mirror, and what he saw had him racing from the room for Ross's toolbox. He returned to find his bed vacant. Thank all of the deities, he wanted no witnesses for what he needed to do. His previous admission had been mortification enough.

Wren started to come into the bathroom but he hollered at him to go away and slammed the door in his face.

He'd just about given up his quest when Ross pounded on the now locked bathroom door. "Open up or so help me God I'll kick this door in."

Nels jerked the door open.

"What in the fuck are you doing?" Ross asked. "Wren said you're cutting yourself. You're bleeding."

"I'm trying to remove the jewelry Farrid gave me. The bastard didn't make these rings so they could be taken off without some sort of cutting tool. I don't want to set off airport sensors every time I travel. The wire clippers slipped and I cut myself. My hands are shaking too much. I need these reminders off me. Can you help me? I just need them...."

Ross held out his hand for the wire cutter in Nels's

hand. "Come over to the bed and lie down before you keel over. I'll do it, but I need you still while I'm working."

He didn't think his mood could get any worse, but having Ross move from nipple to nipple snipping and sliding the gold and aquamarine ring out put him in mortification hell.

When he started to work on his navel ring, Nels dared to open his eyes and sucked in a breath. Ross gazed down at him with such heat in his eyes, it couldn't have been disgust. If he didn't know the man better, he would've said lust. His inner Puritan popped up to remind him he was a sick fuck.

"There, that's got it." Ross stepped away from the bed.

Nels turned his head away and whispered, "I wish to God that were true. You missed one." He slid his hand down and flattened his dick against his body, showing the penile decoration, and closed his eyes again.

"Um, okay. You're going to have to hold extra still for this one."

Nels wanted Thor to magically appear and strike the ground so he could disappear into the bowels of the earth, because he couldn't hide the hard on caused by Ross's touch as he worked on removing the gold ornament. He petitioned any Norse god powerful enough to strike him dead and end his misery.

The gods didn't choose to grant his request, but his embarrassment ended when Ross finished removing Farrid's twisted present and went to the bathroom, returning with a tube of antibiotic cream.

"You need to apply this to all of the, um, areas. You might consider keeping the stones. From what I've seen in the bazaars of Afghanistan, they're top quality aquamarines. You could use them for...for...."

Ross left, and Nels curled into a tight ball and wished he'd never left Denmark. He calmed a bit when Wren spooned his body into his, and held him until his nervous exhaustion put his lights out.

# Chapter Fifteen

"Hey, Nels, this came for you. It's from Denmark." Wren tossed the thick, legal-size envelope at him on his way to raid the refrigerator.

Nels didn't want to touch the official summons. It signified the end of his freedom. Maybe he wouldn't feel so out of control if he returned home. Going to work meant rising early, dressing, driving to work, seeing the same people day after day. With any luck, the routine would put him into a coma, a blessed state of numbness. But, deep in his soul, he knew he'd go mad if day after day turned into year after year.

He fled to his studio as if hell hounds pursued him, for losing himself in his painting had become his refuge. The quick glance he'd had of the enclosed first class airline ticket told him he had two days to finish what he'd started.

Done with just enough time to say his farewells, Nels signed the large canvas with his name, Nels Rainer Kirkegaard. He'd felt compelled to leave something of himself behind. Something not tainted by his kidnapping. He realized he'd been stalling when he cleaned a brush for the second time. He needed to say goodbye to Wren, and he didn't know what to say, but he knew he would never forgive him if he disappeared without a last farewell. But his leave-taking with Ross would be the briefest he could make it. He had given him space after his meltdown, and Nels hadn't known how to bridge the gap.

He stopped at Wren's doorway and watched him sleep. His artist's eye took in the changes in the man since Ross rescued them. More defined cheekbones, wider chest, muscular biceps, and honest-to-God beard stubble on his face, but the faint smile on Wren's lips told him the imp he'd come to love hadn't disappeared altogether.

Nels stepped inside and ran a finger down Wren's cheek. "Wake up., I need to talk to you."

"What's the matter? Are you okay?"

"I'm fine, but I wanted to say goodbye. I'm leaving tomorrow morning, and I don't want to make a big deal of it."

"Leaving? Where are you going? When are you coming back? Does Ross know?"

"I'm going back to Denmark. Do you remember me telling you about my grandfather leaving me his furniture business? I have to go back and run the company. I'm not sure when I'll be back. It'll take some time for me to learn the business as well as I should, and, no, Ross doesn't know. I plan on telling him right before I leave. I detest long goodbyes."

Wren scooted to the middle of his bed before he asked, "Would you do me one last favor before you go?"

"Anything. Just name it."

"Hold me until I fall asleep. I won't do anything I shouldn't, but I miss having you hold me the way we used to fall asleep. For old times' sake?"

Nels removed his shirt and jeans and crawled into bed. He kissed Wren's cheek as he gathered him into his arms. "It will be my pleasure. Be well. Trust Ross. Study hard but take the time to enjoy school and meet new people."

Before Wren rolled over to let him spoon him, he said, "You will come back to us Nels. You will or we'll come get you."

\*\*\*

As Nels thought it would, the aroma of brewed coffee lured Ross from his bedroom. The smile on Ross's face turned into a frown when he spotted his duffel bag on the floor

"Going somewhere, Nels?"

"Yes, I've received my summons to come home. I turned thirty the day before you rescued me."

"Jesus, Nels. I don't know whether to wish you a Happy Birthday or say I'm sorry for the fucking way you spent it. Have you told Wren?"

"We said our goodbyes last night." Nels reached into his jacket pocket and removed a bulky envelope. Here's the title and keys to the Ducati. Wren's nineteenth birthday is next month and I want him to have the bike. I know you'll make a good driver out of him. I've left a token of my friendship for you up in the studio. Don't move it for a couple of weeks until it dries."

Ross leaned against the island as he asked, "What time does your flight leave?"

"In four hours."

"Let me throw on some clothes and I'll drive you to the airport."

*God this is harder than I imagined it would be.* "Thank you, Ross, but I've already called a cab." The sound of a honking horn almost made him weak-kneed with relief. He wanted the hell out of Ross's house before he did something to embarrass himself like loosen the hold he had on the waterworks.

Ross shocked him when he wrapped him in a tight embrace, but the kiss on his cheek left him speechless.

"We'll miss you, Nels. I've enjoyed having you for a friend. Come back to us if you can. The door will always be open to you. Please feel free to call and I'll give you updates on Wren's progress."

Nels had to clear his throat before answering. "I'd like that, Ross. Goodbye friend." And he left as if the denizens of hell pursued him.

\*\*\*

Ross poured himself a cup of coffee in the quiet kitchen and took a healthy sip. He rushed to the sink and spat it out. Aargh, Nels never could make a decent cup of coffee. The thought his friend would not be around to try and get it right had him banging his head into the cabinet over the sink. Great, a bitter thought to go with the bitter taste in his mouth. Ross pulled the plug on the percolator and headed for a shower.

Fully groomed, and not in the least hungry, Ross thought about heading to the store for a paper but couldn't work up the energy until he remembered Nels's mention of a gift left in the third floor studio.

Ross stood rooted to the spot in front of the easel. The forest scene he'd first glimpsed in charcoal outline had grown into a birch forest in full leaf. *Nels, you are one talented bastard. You should be painting full time, not selling furniture. My God, your painting draws me into it. It feels like I'm standing right in the middle of the forest.*

Ross knew the perfect spot for Nels's gift. He'd hang it on the wall opposite his bed. It would be the first thing he saw when he opened his eyes each morning.

Another canvas leaning up against the studio wall drew his eye. Nels had painted Wren leaning against the Ducati with his arms crossed over his chest, and his booted feet crossed in a casual waiting pose. Nels had painted Wren not as he presently looked, but as he would appear when he reached full maturity. *Ah Nels, Wren is going to slay hearts right and left.*

Ross turned the picture to the wall, he'd keep it hidden until he had it framed to give it to Wren as his birthday present.

As he turned to leave, Ross spotted Nels's sketch pad on the leather chaise and sat down to see what, if anything, the artist had left behind. The last sketch forced his breath out in a harsh gasp. His eyes widened at the nude portrait of Nels where he lay propped on one arm on the rug, the Tree of Life. His other hand

238

extended palm up in invitation. The only color in the portrait was the Arctic blue of his eyes.

The impact of the drawing doubled him over in pain, and hot and cold chills racked his body. Ross didn't know how long he rocked back and forth before he felt strong enough to close the cover of the pad and carry it downstairs where he collapsed on the great room rug.

Wren entered wearing nothing but boxer briefs and stopped. "We do have sofas, Ross. Don't you think you'd be more comfortable on one of them instead of lying on the floor?"

"Perhaps."

"Okaay, not to ask a dumb question or anything, but why are you lying on the floor?"

"Because I'm fucking clueless."

"Did you and Nels fight before he left?"

"No. Why would you think so?"

"Because you hardly ever swear. What makes you think you're fucking clueless?"

"Someone had to draw me a picture before I knew what was happening right under my nose. Now, it's too late to do anything about it."

Seeing Wren's eyes sharpen with interest, Ross stood up and gave him a push in the direction of his bedroom. "Get dressed. I'm in the mood for waffles. We'll go to the diner on the corner and pig out."

Ross wished he could say he and Wren settled into a routine after Nels left, but could controlled chaos be called a routine? His business surged, thanks to the sterling references from Morgan, Prinz, and Bristol. Wren kept his appointments with Dr. Lewandowski, and as Nels predicted, he passed his SATs and got into George Mason. At least he wanted to stay close. He wasn't ready to lose another friend so soon.

Wren managed his office when he was on a case and proved to be an efficient executive assistant. Thanks to him, bills got paid on time, Ross didn't miss appointments, and clients left his office happy with the personal attention they received from Wren. They made a good team.

The fly in the ointment floated to the surface in the rare quiet times he had when Wren went out with his new college friends. At such times he gravitated to the former studio and sat on the chaise to curse himself, yet again, for not picking up on what the Dane had been trying to tell him. The one time Nels called, he hadn't been home and Wren relayed his greetings. He couldn't decide if he felt regret or relief for not hearing his voice again.

Another Saturday night. and Wren had abandoned him in favor of a movie with friends. He'd once again wandered up to Nels's studio, but the sound of a ringing phone sent him flying down the stairs. Whoever it was must really want to talk to him because he didn't catch it until the answering machine started to kick in. "Ross here," he barked into the phone.

"Yo, Dawg. Are you breathless because you've got a friend sleeping over and I've interrupted something, or has Tomodashi kicked your ass again?"

"Neither one, Troll. I ran down a flight of steps to catch the phone. What can I do for you?"

"You can get your ass in gear and join me for a few brewskies at the pub. I'm on my way back from visiting my folks in Pennsylvania, and I thought I'd swing by and see how you're doing."

"Sounds good, Troll. See ya in ten. Don't do anything to get yourself evicted from the place in the meantime."

Ross penned a note to Wren and grabbed his keys and headed out. The long, boring evening had just resolved itself.

It was good to see Troll again. After being mauled by his exuberant greeting, Ross caught up on changes in training, equipment, and unclassified operations, and had settled into enjoying his second beer when Troll asked, "So how are Wren and Nels? I'm surprised you didn't bring Nels with you. I hope you know my invitation included him as well."

Ross made rings with his glass on the cardboard coaster for a few seconds before answering. "Wren's fine. He's settled into college quite well and has quite the flock of friends to hang with. The guy's turned into an intelligent young man and can balance working in my office, going to classes, and partying without letting his grades slip.

"Believe it or not, he's pretty grounded. I haven't had to hold his head over the toilet since his first and only experience with one-too-many beers, and even then he had sense enough not to drive his bike but called me to come get him. I'd be lying if I said I did the same at his age."

Troll snickered. "Ah yes, with age comes wisdom or greater capacity to imbibe without puking. And what's Nels up to?"

Ross developed a sudden interest in the travel posters of Ireland hanging behind Troll. "I don't know. I haven't spoken to him since he went back to Denmark."

Troll reached across the table and thunked him right between the eyes.

"Dammit, Lassie. You fucked it up, didn't you?"

"What the hell are you talking about, Troll? What did I fuck up?"

"You let Nels get away without telling him how you felt."

Ross sat ramrod straight in his chair and glared at his friend. "What are you getting at?"

Troll didn't answer until he scanned the tables around them, and assured himself no one had the slightest interest in their conversation. Still, he leaned over and spoke softly. "Come on, Lassie, the looks passing between you two would've melted steel. How could you let him walk out of your life? You've always been buttoned up pretty tight, but damn, you should've loosened up a little in this case."

Ross went pale.

"Lassie, I know. Come on. I'm a special operator. I'm trained to observe."

Sweat trickle down the back of his neck. "Does anyone else know?"

"Do you mean besides the team? No, no one else knows."

He put his face in his hands and groaned, but

stopped trying to hide when his friend nudged him on the arm.

"All of us have known for quite a while now. We're okay with it." Troll laughed. "I'd like to see anyone dumb enough to insult you. Gunner is good with the long gun, and Otter can disassemble humans as easily as a mechanic can a car, and I'm good at strategy and tactics, but you, Lassie, you're good at the close-in fighting. None of us would take you on in hand-to-hand. We've seen your Ginzu knife work. You've kept your preferences on the QT and far away from the flag pole, so we gave you the respect you deserve."

"So why are you bringing this up now, Troll?"

"Because you sometimes need to be hit between the eyes with the obvious. None of us had ever seen you show the slightest emotion around another man before. With Nels, sparks flew whenever you occupied the same space. I thought he'd be making your place his permanent residence by now. Why hasn't he? Did you do something to scare him off?"

Ross' laced his words with exasperation. "No, I didn't do anything to scare him off. I didn't do anything at all. And the sad truth is, I never realized he had any feelings for me at all until the morning he left."

"Geez, Lassie, for such a smart man you can be fucking stupid at times. Why haven't you gone after him?"

"I don't know. There are times I almost convince myself to hop a flight over there and then I back off."

"Are you seeing anyone else?"

Ross reared back as if smacked before admitting, "I've gone on a few dates, but I can't get with the whole dating scene. It's like he took a piece of me with him. I've come to the conclusion I'm wasting my time, so I've stopped dating."

"Maybe you've stopped dating because you already found the one you want?"

"Finding and keeping are not the same. Nels had some serious psychological issues when he left. He hadn't been sleeping well, and he refused to seek counseling for what happened to him in Saudi Arabia. I hope he's doing so in Denmark."

"Well you could always hop a plane and find out."

Ross leaned forward and lowered his voice. "I'm afraid if I show up and tell him what I feel, he'll...he'll.... Ah hell, I don't know what he'll do. What I do know is, I'm not going to make the first move. If he wants me, he'll have to come get me. Maybe this time he'll spell it out in big letters or draw me another picture."

"*Another* picture, huh? Well, I wish you luck, Lassie. Finish your beer and then I think it's time you got yourself home."

Troll gave him his usual exuberant hug and back slap in the parking lot. Nothing appeared to have changed with the way his former teammate felt about him.

# Chapter Sixteen

Nels's head spun like a top. Three meetings so far this morning, and the last one with the budget team had given him a sour stomach and a splitting headache. He'd sat through the discussion of the bottom line with a look of interest glued to his face.

The team his grandfather had chosen to run the company while he played rich playboy this last year had been more than efficient, but the same couldn't be said of their boss. He'd yet to summon any enthusiasm for the job, although, as the three meetings this morning proved, he hid it quite well.

Maybe if he could get two consecutive nights of dream-free sleep, his attitude would change, but, until it happened, he'd keep a tight hold on his impatience. Yep, he'd turned into a functioning hypocrite, and, as courses of action went, he knew how to do that very well.

Nels interrupted his self-flagellation to answer the phone. Knowing his mother was on the other end of the line didn't improve his headache.

"Nels, my friend Marta tells me you turned down

her invitation to dinner last week."

"Yes, Mother, I did. I'm too busy at the moment learning how to run this company to spend my weekends making small talk at dinner parties."

"Nels, you've been home six months now, and I know you aren't a slow learner. I also know Marta wanted you to meet her daughter. Dagmar is a successful lawyer. It's unfortunate her first marriage didn't take, but thank God they didn't have children, and, being a lawyer, she retained all the property."

Nels wanted to bang the phone's receiver on his desk until his mother took the hint and hung up. "Mother, I have no interest in meeting Dagmar."

"It's time you lived up to your responsibilities to this family. You need to take your place in our social circles, to get married and start a family."

"Still not interested. I prefer to make my own friends."

"I will not take no for an answer. I'm having a small gathering of friends for dinner this weekend, and you will be there. I've invited Marta and Dagmar. Now stop closeting yourself in your apartment and leave off daubing paint on canvas long enough to socialize with the right people."

Nels saw nothing but a wash of red before his

eyes. Rage made him grasp the phone receiver so hard he couldn't believe the plastic didn't crumble. In a voice constricted by his anger, he hissed, "You will have to make my apologies to Marta and Dagmar. I won't be attending your dinner party this weekend or participating in any other matchmaking scheme you come up with in the future. I'll thank you to keep your grand designs out of my life."

He hung up with his mother still spluttering her outrage.

His phone rang an hour later, and he knew who this would be. "Yes, Father?"

"Your mother called to tell me how rude you were to her. You will come to dinner this evening, and we will discuss your attitude."

His father didn't give him a chance to accept or decline before the line went dead. Not surprising. His father held the position of supreme dictator in the Kirkegaard family.

Nels thought about not showing up but let the thought go. His father would storm into his office to upbraid him when it suited him to do so, and he didn't need to air his family's dirty laundry in front of his staff. Now he had a sour stomach, a splitting headache, and simmering rage as companions for what remained of this craptastic day.

***

The maid showed Nels into the library. It made him feel like he'd been called into the headmaster's office for a schoolboy infraction. He found his mother seated by the fireplace, and his father, drink in hand, standing beside her chair. His father commenced the attack before he had a chance to tender a polite greeting.

"Sit down, Nels."

He considered ignoring the terse command, but childish resistance would serve nothing but to prolong the time he had to stay before he could get the hell out of this parents' presence. He had no intention of eating dinner with them this evening. The time he'd bend to his father's will had come to an end.

"I see you're still wearing those ridiculous bow ties. At least the suit is suitably tailored."

"Thank you, Father. I'll be sure to pass the compliment on to my tailor."

Wynter set his glass down on the mantle and pointed at him. "You'll lose your disrespectful tone of voice and apologize to your mother for your behavior

250

this morning."

Nels crossed his legs before facing off with his father. "No, I don't think I will. I don't account it rude to ask someone to stop making arrangements without first consulting me. Mother scheduled her dinner party without calling to verify my schedule. If she'd bothered to do so, I could have told her I'm too busy at the moment, and can't attend." He lifted his chin. "I find it curious I've been home for six months, and this is the first time I've been invited to dine with my parents. It hasn't escaped me the invitation came as a result of your need to castigate me like a schoolboy for some imagined infraction."

Nels steeled himself for his father's response.

"Now you listen here, Nels, you have obligations to this family—"

"You can't say it, can you?"

"Say what? Your name?"

"No, you can't say what I am to you. Son. I'm your son, and I've just realized you've never called me that. It's always been Nels. I'm thirty years old now, Father, and I no longer need to hear you call me son, and I sure as hell no longer need to listen to your dictates." He drew a breath and plowed on. "You and Mother have never shown the slightest interest in my life except to pay the bills for boarding school on time, so your sudden interest in me seems strange. Do you even know or care what I did in the year I spent abroad?"

Wynter Kirkegaard tossed back his drink and put it down on a convenient silver tray. "I'd imagine you spent it on wine, women, and song. I'm still furious with your grandfather for putting such a ridiculous stipulation in his will. It's immaterial, now. You're back, and you need to make the correct connections to be accepted in society. We'll not have a wastrel in this family."

Nels ignored his father's jibe and turned to his mother. "My recent travels might interest you, Mother. I made some outstanding friends in America. I also had the misfortune to meet some very bad people, elsewhere. You see, I met a man by the name of Ross de Lassy, and he hired me to help restore his home. I think even you'd approve of Ross. He can trace his family history to the Battle of Hastings in 1066. His family helped William the Conqueror defeat the Anglo-Saxon ruler of England." Nels chose to take his mother's lack of response as encouragement to continue. "Ross had recently retired from the Army where he'd served as a Green Beret or in special operations, and he'd started his own investigative service. I had no idea, when I agreed to help him remodel his new home, I'd find myself in desperate need of his services. You see, I'd gone to a local bookstore and a sex slave ring kidnapped me right off the street in Alexandria, Virginia, and sold me to a Saudi Arabian. Did you know my silver blond hair and blue eyes are much prized in the Middle East?"

Freya Kirkegaard broke her silence to castigate her recalcitrant son. "Nels, if you're trying to shock us with this sordid little fabrication of yours, you can stop."

"Fabrication, Mother? Oh no. I'd never lie about something like this. It's all true. In fact, I'd still be there servicing a rich, perverted Arab, if Ross hadn't found me and rescued me.

"There was another man being held captive with me. His name is Wren, and he'd been a sex slave since he was eleven. It was his job to teach me the sexual techniques our owner desired. To give him his due, he taught me things I would never have learned living here."

"*Enough*," Wynter Kirkegaard roared as he crossed the room and jerked Nels from the chair. "I will not have you spewing such filth in front of your mother. You'll not return to this house until you can apologize for your behavior."

Nels straightened the lay of his suit. "Apologize for my behavior? I was kidnapped, held prisoner, tortured, and coerced to do things against my will, and I'm the one who needs to apologize for speaking of it? Your parental compassion overwhelms me, Father."

Wynter Kirkegaard rounded on his wife. "This is the result of that ridiculous stipulation your father put in his will."

Nels continued before his mother could respond to her husband's accusation. "You needn't worry my previous misfortune will taint your precious standing in Copenhagen society, because it'll be a cold day in hell before I return here again. Until this moment, I've striven to be a dutiful son, to earn your love, but I don't need or want your love, anymore.'

Wynter shot back, "And what about our money? You've never turned your nose up at our social position before. You've had it easy all of your life because of our wealth."

Nels let his shoulders droop as he faced his father. "It's a sad day when you learn neither one of your parents has even an iota of love to give you, but after what happened to me this summer, I don't want to waste what remains of my life on a useless quest for parental love. Here's a suggestion, Father, put a stipulation in your own will that you have no son to inherit your wealth.

"So good night, goodbye, and don't bother to call me ever again."

Nels's rage evaporated as soon as he turned the lights on in the large rooms he called home in the upper story of his factory. Most times, the sight of his grandfather's hand-built furniture soothed him, but not this evening. As he cast his eyes around, it struck him he hadn't had time to put a personal stamp on the place, but his easel stood front and center. He'd sketched the bare outlines of a sea scene but hadn't gotten much farther.

He needed to get out of the constricting suit and pour himself a large glass of brandy. As he removed his cufflinks and opened the wooden chest he used as a jewel box, his eye fell on the cardboard box containing the knife Ross had given him. He slammed the box shut and walked into the closet to hang up his suit.

The first sip of brandy had made it down his throat when the image of the knife popped back into his mind, and he returned to his jewel box. His hand trembled as he lifted the lid, and he cursed himself for his cowardice. Snatching the small box from the chest, Nels carried it to one of the leather chairs by his unlit fireplace.

Setting the snifter down, Nels removed the knife from its box and opened the blade. He inhaled sharply when a fine line of blood appeared on his thumb. He shouldn't have been surprised at its sharpness. Ross hadn't given him a toy. It was designed to cut. It was ready to cut, and he was ready to be cut.

As the seductiveness of the thought began to overwhelm him, Nels flung himself out of the chair and began pacing the room. It'd be no great loss, after all. He had no one, abso-fucking no one to miss him. His former parents might even be relieved after what he'd done this evening.

Nels held the knife point over the middle of his left wrist. The unexpected intrusion of a ringing phone startled him enough to drop it. He didn't want to answer, but the work habits ingrained in him by his grandfather made him hesitate. Maybe something had happened in the factory.

Nels returned to his chair and picked up the phone, "*Hej*?" When he recognized the voice on the other end, tears spilled from his eyes.

"Wren, what's wrong? It must be six o'clock in the morning there?"

"I got dumped by Sally last night. She's dating a senior. I guess she prefers older men."

"Ah, to paraphrase one of your American songwriters, the first cut is indeed the deepest. I didn't realize you cared for Sally so deeply."

Wren laughed, "I didn't either until I got dumped. Maybe I'll stick to men. At least I understand them better."

"I hope you're not waiting for me to choose a course for you. It's your life and no one else's."

Wren chuckled. "Now you sound like Ross. Hey, do you have a cold? You sound kind of hoarse."

"Perhaps I'm coming down with something. I've been working pretty crazy hours. How is Ross? Is his business going well?"

"Yeah, business is booming. As for how he is, ask him yourself. He managed to drag his ass out of bed early this morning to go running."

"No, wait, Wren, no need to bother...." But Wren had already turned the phone over to Ross. His gut clenched when he heard him ask, "How are you?"

"I'm fine. I'm becoming quite the businessman, but the long hours haven't left me much time for recreation."

"I know what you mean. Um, I love the painting you did for me. I've hung it in my bedroom."

At the mention of his bedroom, Nels had to listen all the harder over the roaring in his ears. He almost missed the next exchange.

"We miss you. Um... I miss you."

Do it, he told himself. Man up and do it. "I miss you, too, Ross."

He waited through a long, pregnant count before Ross spoke again. "Here's Wren. He wants to ask you something. Take care, Nels."

"When are you coming back, Nels?"

"I don't know. Maybe I'll show up for your graduation."

"No way. I'm not waiting three years to see you again, so don't make me spend some of the money Ross invested for me for a plane ticket over there to drag you back. You heard Ross, he misses you, and so do I."

Wren's call had added the final straw to break the camel's back, and so he lied. "Uh, someone is trying to call me on this line. I'll talk to you soon. Be well."

Nels ended the connection, and when he moved to return to his chair, his foot hit the knife he'd dropped.

Picking it up, he took care to close it and returned it to the box. He downed the remainder of his brandy in one gulp, and moved to his bookcase to take down the phone directory for Copenhagen. He'd make an appointment with the first name he came to. *Ah, Doctor Aagaard it is. Well, Doctor Aagaard, let's see if you're as good as the psychologist Ross uses.*

## Chapter Seventeen

Nels uncrossed his fingers when Wren opened the door and greeted him with a huge grin. He didn't feel up to coming face-to-face with Ross until he had a chance to calm down.

"Well, if it isn't the Templar home from the Crusades. I'd almost come to the conclusion the Saracens had taken you prisoner and hadn't gotten around to demanding ransom."

"You're looking well, Wren."

"I swear to God, Nels, if Ross or I hadn't heard from you by the time summer vacation rolled around, I would've hopped a plane and dragged your ass back here. You've been gone much too long, Nels.

"I missed you and, uh, Ross, as well. Yes, I've been gone far too long."

"Since you didn't give me a chance to thank you before you left, thanks for the Ducati. Best birthday present ever. It's a real babe magnet, and I don't mean just girls."

Nels stepped inside when Wren backed away from the door. "I'm fine, and you're welcome. How are you and Ross getting along? Is he treating you well?"

"I'm doing great, much better than you, it seems. You look like hell, Templar. Aren't you getting any? I'll bet you've forgotten everything I've taught you. You must've because only abstinence leaves such sad lines on a face."

Nels walked into the business office and discovered no one waiting to speak to Ross, so they had the whole first floor to themselves. "I haven't forgotten one iota of what you taught me, Wren."

He stood his ground when Wren walked up to him and bumped his chest, and he put his arms around the nineteen-year-old.

"You've grown taller and filled out since last I saw you. Ross must be feeding you well. Keep it up, and you may grow to be as tall as me."

"Yep, I'm six foot. Ross complains I have the discerning palate of a vacuum, but it's his fault. If he didn't cook such wonderful things, I wouldn't eat so much. The muscles are from a mixed martial arts training program. It was either develop the muscles or let Ross's sensei turn me into sushi."

"Are you still seeing...."

"Yep, I'm still seeing the psychologist Ross set me up with, and I'm taking online classes and day classes at the university. I'm not sure what I want to be when I grow up, but for now, it's either quantum physicist, mechanical engineer, astronomer, or proctologist."

Nels threw back his head and laughed heartily when Wren looked up at him and fluttered his eyelashes at the last career choice.

Wren, who hadn't backed away from the full body contact, cocked his head far enough back to study his face. "Nope, Templar, still not buying it."

"Not buying what, Wren?"

"I don't believe you remember a thing I taught you. If you had, there wouldn't be, despite your laughing at my joke, such sadness in your eyes. You'd be sporting a beautiful woman or perhaps a man on your arm by now. Speaking of women, I really like their breasts, and they have an extra set of lips that are even more fun to kiss."

"Wren, do you remember me teaching you how to construct a filter between your brain and your mouth? I'm thinking you've forgotten my instructions as well."

"Nope, you can't distract me. You haven't answered my question. You have forgotten, haven't you?"

"And I tell you I haven't."

Wren sent his heart stuttering when he looked up

from under his long eyelashes and smiled the smile that always signified mischief about to be made. "There's only one way to prove this, Templar, and you know it."

"Well bring it on, then." It gave him no small measure of satisfaction when Wren gaped at his dare. He didn't protest when Wren's lips covered his. He remembered what the man liked, and cupped his face, and smoothed small circles behind his ears as he deepened the kiss.

When Wren opened for him, he plundered his mouth until he felt him respond, and then he kicked it up a notch.

Time for the big finish, he thought, and ran his tongue over the pulsing vein in his neck, and nipped his way along his jaw before returning to seal his lips with Wren's. He used his other hand to cup Wren, who'd become fully aroused.

As he gave a small squeeze, Wren groaned into his mouth, and Nels released him with a victorious, "I win. First one to moan wins, and you know it. You made the rule, so don't try and weasel out of it."

Wren's eyes sparkled. "Yes, you won fair and square." But his eyes grew serious again, and he tugged Nels closer. "You've no idea, Templar, how much it means to me when you show me love like that. No hesitation, no reservations, and no blame for what you went through."

Nels wrapped his arms around him in reassurance. "You know I love you. We'll always have a special relationship for what we shared, and I'm not talking guilt."

"Yeah, but now you'll love me like the obnoxious little brother you never had."

"No, I'll love you like the beautiful, unique, exotic man who chooses to masquerade as a wren. One of these days, you'll find someone, man or woman, who'll see you the way I do, and they'll be fortunate if you choose to accept their love."

"I can only hope I find someone like you or Ross."

Uncomfortable with the heavy emotion in the room, Nels stepped away and changed the subject. "Is Ross at home?"

"You missed him going upstairs by five minutes. He's taking a shower. At least I hope he is, because he came home a sweaty, smelly mess from the long run he took this morning. Go on up and surprise him like you did me."

Nels climbed two stairs before Wren stopped him. "Are you going to tell him?"

"Tell him what, Wren?" The raspberry sound Wren gave made him smile.

"C'mon Templar, this is me you're speaking to. Have you forgotten how you overcame your aversion to engaging in sex with me?"

"No, but how does that relate to Ross?

"You're going to make me spell it out, aren't you?" He tsked. "When you balked at having me take you with more than my lips, I told you to imagine me as someone else, someone you loved, and you did, and it made me jealous. I envied the woman whose name you called as you came. I wanted someone to love me so much they would call my name in passion, and as we both know, our master would never be the one to do so."

"No, he never would. He loved only himself."

"I discovered who you called for when Ross sent me to fetch a document from his study. I learned I'd been off base by a mile when I read the name on Ross's framed genealogy chart. You hadn't called a woman's name at all, you were calling for him. Ross's real first name, Roslin, is close enough to the Rosalyn I thought I heard." He stepped forward and hugged Nels. "You know, Templar, you have a chance at grabbing the happiness ring here, but you'll never do it unless you stretch out your hand. Go upstairs and put the man out of his misery. He's spent the last year wanting you."

"You're mistaking wanting for pity," Nels rasped. "The way this last year has gone for me, I'd come screaming out of the closet and discover I'd horribly misread his feelings."

Wren stood with arms akimbo. "Your Norman doesn't do pity. He pines for what he wants and didn't dare ask for. He's gone out a few times, but he never brings anyone home, and he doesn't stay out long enough to have more than dinner or a drink."

Nels demurred. "It's still not proof positive he's dating men and not women, Wren."

"Well if it *is* women, I question his taste in them, because they're using aftershave rather than perfume, and they aren't shaving their faces close enough to stop giving him beard burn. After what happened to you, Nels, he won't make a move. It'll have to be your choice alone. Give him a break, Templar. Take a chance and make the first move."

Wren dodged around Nels. "You can tell Ross I'm going out and I won't be back until late tonight, maybe not until tomorrow morning, if I get lucky. If you two do manage to get it on, please do it behind closed doors. I don't want to come upstairs and find the two of you humping like bunnies on the dining room table. Unless you're warming up and waiting for me to complete the threesome."

Wren danced out of range of the swipe he took at him. "Filter, Wren. For God's sake filter. Don't forget to—"

"Yeah, yeah, take a condom. I don't leave home without one, *ever*. And I don't accept condoms from anyone. It's either one I've brought with me or we don't put Tab A into Slot B. I also don't leave home without wallet, keys, and a large, wickedly sharp pocket knife. I swear, if I had to carry one more thing, I'd need a purse."

Wren blew him a kiss and shut the door behind himself, and Nels climbed the stairs. He delayed a moment to enjoy all of the improvements he'd helped make and then followed the sound of running water to Ross's bedroom. The bed drew him, and he toed his loafers off and stretched out on it. As he ran his fingers over the soft fur cover, he closed his eyes to remember the many times he'd dreamed of being in this very spot while imprisoned in the master's harem.

Ross stopped dead at the sight of Nels stretched

out on his bed. If he'd been nude instead of wearing jeans and a V-necked cashmere sweater the same color as his eyes, it would be his nightly dream incarnate.

It took real effort for him to finish towel drying his hair and cross the room to his dresser. He selected a pair of boxer-briefs and stepped into them. Feeling a little less vulnerable, he turned to find Nels sitting on the side of his bed with his head in his hands.

"Is there a problem, Nels?"

"There is. I've come to collect what's owed me."

Ross, who'd been buttoning the shirt he'd chosen to go with jeans, stopped and gawked at him. "Oh my God, in all the excitement of the rescue and getting Wren settled, I never paid you for your help in renovating this place. Let me throw on a pair of jeans and I'll fetch my checkbook."

He felt his heart kick into high gear when Nels bumped chests with him then started unbuttoning his shirt. "I didn't come for a paltry paycheck, Norman."

"What then?"

"I've come to collect the Danegeld, the tribute you owe me."

"And if I refuse to pay it?"

"Well then I'll do what any Viking would. I'll take it by force." With one swift motion, Nels pushed the partially buttoned shirt over Ross's shoulders and trapped his arms.

"Surrender to me, de Lassy."

Ross froze, captured in the eerie polar ice of Nels's eyes until he lowered his lids and sighed, "Yes," and the Dane kissed him for the first time.

He tried to embrace Nels, but the shirt prevented him. "Nels, you need to free my arms if you want me to pay your Danegeld in full."

The buttons flew off and pinged on the floor, and Ross laughed at the remains of his shirt. The Viking had used the most expeditious manner of removing the constraint.

Ross nuzzled Nels's neck and said the words he should've said a year ago. "I want you Nels, I've wanted you since you moved into my guest room."

"Why didn't you ever tell me?"

"When it comes to private and circumspect, you're my equal. I didn't know you had feelings for me as well. But when I searched for clues to your disappearance, and came across the picture you drew of me, I began to hope you might have some feeling for me."

"I had so many feelings for you I was tongue-tied, and we Danes have a hard time displaying our emotions."

"When I saw how withdrawn you were after the rescue I backed off. I thought you needed more time. And then, when I found your sketchpad after you returned to Denmark.... The drawing of you on the rug.... I've been kicking myself for my lousy timing and cluelessness ever since."

Nels lowered his forehead until it touched Ross's. "Okay, I'm going to say this slowly so there'll be no further misunderstandings. I'm not interested in women. I've never been attracted to women, but I've had to keep my sexual preferences hidden. My father would've kicked me out of the house if he knew, and my mother would've devoted all of her energy to reclaiming her father's business, rather than let her abomination of a son have it."

Ross asked, "So why now? What's changed?"

"What has changed is, I no longer give a damn what my parents think, and even though my grandfather wanted me to run Danegeld, it's not for me. I want to paint, Ross. I sold the business to a man who knows more about the factory than I ever will. I've retained a consulting position and a large share of the stock, but everything I need to do can be done from here. Is the third floor studio for rent, by any chance?"

"Perhaps we can work out a deal, Viking. My studio in lieu of the Danegeld." Ross reached under Nels's sweater and ran his hands up his ribcage until he got it over his head and tossed it on the floor. When he reached to unbutton Nels's jeans, his breath hissed out. "You've put the navel ring back in. Why?"

"This one can be removed any time I don't want to wear it. I saw your eyes when you helped me remove it the first time. I'll never forget the heat in them, and I wanted to see it again." He grinned. "Yes, that's it, like molten lava."

Ross knelt and tongued the aquamarine bead, feeling the quiver go through Nels's body. "You're mine, and I don't give back what's mine. I'm finished talking. Let me show you how a de Lassy pays his debts."

When he'd regained sufficient strength in his satiated body, Nels rolled over to face Ross and chuckled. "Does this mean I get my dream of a home with a white picket fence?"

Ross smoothed his hand through the bright gilt of Nels's hair and tweaked it playfully as he deliberated. "A picket fence? Do you think such a fence will look good around the moat of a Norman castle?"

"To put a picket fence around a Norman castle might be quite a challenge."

"Aren't your Viking carpentry skills up to the challenge?"

"Mmm, I believe so, but if not, I have a few other skills you may avail yourself of. In fact, one of them is offering you the use of it right now."

Ross chortled and reached out to play with the small chunk of blue ice he hoped Nels would never remove. He enjoyed feeling the other man turn to putty in his hands each time he tongued it.

"Well I think I need to assess your work first to ensure it's as good as you say. I must confess, I'm a little dissatisfied with the historical inaccuracy and structural proportions of the picture you drew of me as a knight."

"Inaccuracies? I hold a PhD in history. There are no historical inaccuracies in my drawing, and my proportions are spot on."

"Sorry, but you're wrong." Ross left the bed and went to the bottom drawer of his dresser and removed the drawing in question. Returning, he pointed to the contested area, "See, it's inaccurate."

"Inaccurate? It's a penis and balls. How can those

be historically inaccurate?"

"Come on, Doctor Kirkegaard, even I know Norman knights weren't circumcised."

When Nels huffed in consternation, Ross interrupted him. "As to proportions, I think you need some tactile experience to get it right." He took Nels's hands and placed them on his package. "As you can now feel, your proportions were a bit on the skimpy side."

"Ah, *Monseigneur* de Lassy. I beg your forgiveness. Yes, you're quite right. Norman knights didn't practice circumcision, but I've always felt historically accurate renderings make uncircumcised penises appear like the artist took the easy way out. A formless tube of flesh doesn't convey the power of that organ."

"I'd have to agree."

"As to proportion, perhaps the water in the pond I drew him leaving was cold. Furthermore, even though I have an eidetic memory, I still need to see the object first to be able to draw it with any degree of accuracy. Until today, I'd never seen you nude. I'll be happy to correct my errors of proportion. Shall I fetch my eraser?"

Nels had been stroking him the entire time, and

the question made him groan. "No, not now, by all that's right with this world, not now. Besides, there's more of me you need to see. I have a fine back, which you failed to capture in the original drawing."

Nels pushed him until he rolled over. "Do you mean here?" The perverse Viking ran his tongue over the nape of his neck. "Or maybe you mean here," he whispered as he kissed the two dimples at the base of his spine.

Nels had the audacity to grin like a Cheshire cat when he had to clear his voice before answering his questions. "You're getting closer, but you need to explore lower. I think the cheeks of my ass are the best feature of my posterior side. I've worked hard to achieve such firm proportions, and I wouldn't want you to do them a disservice, should you draw them."

"I'd never stint on rendering such beauty."

Ross turned, the better to see his eyes. "You aren't just saying that?"

"No. It will be my pleasure to draw you as God made you."

"Then show me. I place all of me in your hands, Nels. My body is your living canvas, make of it a masterpiece."

"It will be my life's work, Ross. But for this

meisterwerk, I'll need to use a different medium."

Ross cradled his head in his bent arm. "I thought you preferred to work in oils. What'll you use this time, watercolor?"

"Yes, I prefer oils, but this time neither oils nor watercolors nor pen and ink will do."

"What's left then, crayons?" His smile evaporated when Nels used one finger to trace around his nipple and down each ridge of his abdomen until he reached his navel, where he traced a continuous, slow circle. He sucked in a breath, and his muscles hardened at the sensual caress.

"You're getting warmer de Lassy. For this portrait, I'll be using...finger paints. Now, hold that pose while I prepare my canvas."

**Sign up for the Decadent Publishing Newsletter here** http://eepurl.com/SQ75f **and never miss stories like:**

# Chapter One

An innocent hug, a brief touch of a soft, feminine body to his hard chest and Orion closed his eyes, wishing he could hold the woman to him for just one second more as she protested his early departure. But he looked over her shoulder, and the scene in the backyard barbecue disturbed him. The grass had faded to a sickly green, and the voices calling encouragement to the men playing horseshoes sounded muted and distorted. Orion stiffened, pasted a polite grin on his face, and murmured his good-bye to the hostess.

The acrid aroma of unclaimed hot dogs turning to charcoal on the backyard grill followed him as he put one foot in front of the other to get to his truck, and, once inside the cab, he ignored the impulse to push the gas pedal to the floor. Peeling out would call attention to his hasty departure. He didn't need an audience. They might ask him questions he couldn't answer.

The Great Spirit must've been smiling down upon him, for he spotted the dirt road in time to take it and park before the isolated road in Jacksonville, North Carolina, disappeared and the brown, dusty hills of Afghanistan took its place. Gunnery Sergeant Orion Brown turned off the ignition and opened a window to dissipate the odor of AVGAS. It made the *whop, whop, whop* of slowing chopper blades all the louder, and he clenched and unclenched his fists to stop them from shaking like a junkie's going through detox.

The smell of burnt oil wrinkled his nose. The cordite on the lance corporal's cammies filled his nostrils while the guy sobbed and clung to him, not giving a fuck about maintaining a macho posture. Orion glanced over the corporal's shoulder and caught the corpsman closing the eyes of the Marine he'd been working on. He'd participated in this maneuver enough times to know what came next. He touched the sleeve of his uniform, and his fingers came away wet with the corporal's tears. Another Marine killed in combat, and his shoulder used for solace.

His gut twisted at the necessity of bucking up another man to face battle without his battle buddy covering his six, and his mouth puckered at the unexpectedly bitter taste of the words he murmured in consolation, but this time his soothing words fell on deaf ears. The Marine who'd sought a measure of comfort for his grief couldn't hear him. The cessation of sobs, and the stillness of the lance corporal's body, sent a zing of fear through him, and he patted the man's cheek. No response. The lance corporal hadn't stopped crying, he'd stopped breathing.

"Corpsman! Goddamn it, help me. This Marine's wounded as well."

His fear made his voice loud and shrill, and everyone in the chopper, who'd been so busy tending the obviously wounded Marine, froze in place. Orion forgave them the startled looks, for no one, himself included, realized the Marine who'd carried his friend to safety had also been wounded and bled out while he cried. Orion ducked his head into the lance corporal's shoulder, and, just this once, sought his own comfort as he rocked the fallen Marine.

He let the corpsman take the body from his arms, but the relief of the weight, strangely, brought unexpected pain. Orion rubbed the center of his chest and had the surreal thought that this was what it felt like when your heart hit rock bottom. He never held anything back, be it giving comfort, or support or advice, so he shouldn't be surprised to find his emotional reservoir empty. Gunnery Sergeant Orion Brown had nothing left to give, and his heart had just free-fallen to hit the rock bottom of an empty well. It made the same damn questions echo all the louder in his mind.

*What the fuck am I doing wrong? How can I keep my men safe? I've taught them everything I know. What else is there?*

The hard plastic of the steering wheel cutting into his forehead as he slumped against it, and a yell from someone in a passing car to find an actual parking lot if he wanted to sleep in his truck, brought Orion back to North Carolina.

He checked his rearview mirror before putting the truck in gear, and caught his reflection. Yep, same poker-faced expression. He wore it pretty much 24/7 now. He'd developed it especially for visiting the psychologist because, while he might be crazy, no one ever had a reason to call him stupid. If he even hinted at his nightly thoughts of terminating himself, he'd either be a guest in a VA psych ward or a drugged-up zombie. Nope, not happening...at least not today.